"LAY OFF THAT GUN!
I'LL BREAK YOUR ARM!"

Weston yelled. He hauled with savage passion, meaning to disable Blanding. But the saddle girth broke, and the tremendous force of Stanley's onslaught swung Blanding clear of the horse. He let go of Blanding and clipped him a hard blow on the chin.

They were both quick, Stanley bounding erect, but Blanding jerking up only far enough to lean on his left hand. His right swept out with the gun.

"—— —— you, Weston!" he hissed in deadly calm. "You'll never slug another man!"

Suddenly they all grew mute. Blanding was deliberate. This was self-defense. His big white jaw stood out, his hair stood up. His eyes were diabolical. He steadied the gun, lining it up with Stanley's body. Suddenly, a shot cracked out. . . .

Books by Zane Grey

Arizona Ames
The Arizona Clan
Black Mesa
The Border Legion
Boulder Dam
The Call of the Canyon
Code of the West
The Deer Stalker
Desert Gold
Drift Fence
Forlorn River
The Fugitive Trail
The Hash Knife Outfit
The Heritage of the Desert
Horse Heaven Hill
Knights of the Range
The Light of the Western Stars
Lone Star Ranger
Lost Pueblo
The Lost Wagon Train
The Man of the Forest

The Mysterious Rider
Raiders of Spanish Peaks
The Rainbow Trail
Rawhide Justice
Robbers' Roost
Rogue River Feud
Shadow on the Trail
Stranger from the Tonto
Sunset Pass
Thunder Mountain
To the Last Man
The Trail Driver
Twin Sombreros
Under the Tonto Rim
The U.P. Trail
Valley of Wild Horses
Wanderer of the Wasteland
Western Union
West of the Pecos
Wilderness Trek
Wyoming

Published by POCKET BOOKS

ZANE GREY

HORSE HEAVEN HILL

PUBLISHED BY POCKET BOOKS NEW YORK

Cover art by Murray Tinkleman

POCKET BOOKS, a Simon & Schuster division of
GULF & WESTERN CORPORATION
1230 Avenue of the Americas, New York, N.Y. 10020

Copyright © 1959 by Zane Grey, Inc.

Published by arrangement with Harper & Row, Publishers, Inc.

ISBN: 0-671-82932-7

First Pocket Books printing December, 1964

15 14 13 12 11 10 9 8 7

Trademarks registered in the United States and other countries.

Printed in the U.S.A.

HORSE HEAVEN HILL

1

THAT NORTHERN section of the state of Washington, as far as the ranch land was concerned, encroached upon wild country, the margin of civilization, the rolling sage plains, blue as the sky, which terminated in a mountain called Horse Heaven Hill.

Viewed from the Wade ranch house, from a knoll overlooking the thriving town, the open country spread like a fan to the north and west. The gray expanse merged in the blue, without any barren patches, and spread away, soon to heave into mounds and hills, timber-topped and shaggy, which waved onto the range of mountains. Out beyond somewhere rolled the great Oregon, mighty river of the Northwest. The scene had all the austere beauty characteristic of this north country when uncultivated. South of the little city the sage had given way to wheat. Here Wadestown was the most northerly outpost, located on the railroad that ran almost east and west, and which served as the border line of the wilderness.

Far out on the sunny reaches tiny black dots and clouds of dust furnished telltale signs of riders. They might have been driving cattle, but considering the absence of any cattle in the wide foreground this was doubtful to experienced eyes. Moreover, it was wild-horse country.

Horse Heaven Hill towered on the Clespelem Indian Reservation. The wild mustangs were wilder than deer and they were the property of the Indians. Thousands of these horses had roamed the sage country unmolested for years. Usually bands of a hundred or less, under the leadership of a stallion, ran together, working down out of the mountains in the fall, and returning the next summer when the springs dried up in the low country. Seldom did the Indians chase these wild horses, except occasionally to trap one of the beautiful stallions. They were as free as the waving sage. Their range extended over the mountains to the swift Oregon. They grazed and lolled and raced and fought, and foaled their colts in peace, and lived the lives of eagles.

But the time came when this tranquil existence was rudely disrupted. Abe Wade, rancher of that section, attracted by the strong demand for cattle, rounded up most of his stock and sold them. The unprecedented move left his cowboys with more leisure than was good for them. Hurd Blanding, lately from the ranges of Wyoming, originated a scheme with young Ellery Wade, ne'er-do-well son of the rancher, which set the whole community by the ears. With a selected outfit of hard-riding cowboys and a force of Clespelem Indians, they chased and trapped three thousand head of wild horses, and by a trick called tailing, which was simply tying the tail of one horse to the head of another, they drove the whole band to the railroad and shipped them to Montana to be slaughtered for chicken feed. Blanding paid the Clespelems one dollar a head for their assistance in making the drive; he gave young Wade one thousand and divided a like sum among the cowboys. As it soon leaked out that he had received three dollars a head it was clear he had made a large sum of money for a cowboy.

The substance of this singular news came to Lark Burrell the very day she arrived at Wadestown, to make her home with the Wades.

Lark was a second cousin of Marigold Wade, who had prevailed upon her father to offer a home to their orphan relative. Lark was eighteen. Most of her life she had lived in Idaho, far south on the great ranges of a still unfenced desert country. Burrell, her father, had owned a big stretch of land there, wild land which no one but Lark considered worth anything. He left it to her along with a ramshackle cabin, a fine stream of water, a few head of stock, and a drove of wild mustangs. Lark had come honestly by her love of wild horses. She had been brought up among them. She herself was like an untamed colt. But much as she desired it, she could no longer live on the profitless ranch, with only an old herder. So when the Wades sent for her, she was grateful and accepted the home offered, feeling in her heart that someday she would return to Idaho.

Lark had been given a room that opened out upon the sage country, with the strangely named mountain dark on the horizon. At once this view struck her. It was not barren or big enough to resemble her country; still it charmed her. And the hour soon came when she sat in her window seat, consumed by the news she had heard downstairs. Three thousand head of wild horses sold for chicken feed!

The shock to Lark was something that could not have been understood by most people. Marigold's rich laugh had pealed out. "Look at the kid's face!" Lark had fled to her room, and there she had ventured to peep in her mirror. It was a stormy, revealing face. She flung herself away, and, curling in the window seat, she tried to realize an appalling thing. *"Three thousand head of wild horses sold for chicken feed!"* Lark repeated, until she got its meaning through her head.

Then her tears flowed so that she could not see the sage plains and the beckoning mountain.

But they were soon burned away. All at once she hated this handsome cousin, Ellery Wade, who had kissed her and made much of her upon her arrival. It was at dinner, after she had unpacked and donned the only nice dress she owned, that the disturbance had come. Ellery had burst in upon the family wildly elated, his pockets bulging with money, to which he called attention by vociferous word and violent action. Right there Lark had divined he was a spoiled child, the only son of the family. Marigold had shrieked at the sight of the money and flashed her greedy white hands for it. Mr. Wade, after his surprise, had showed interest and pleasure. The boy's mother had seemed nonplused.

"Hurd sold the whole blooming bunch of wild horses," Ellery had shouted. "My share was—well, never mind."

"Where—how'd he sell them?" his father had asked curiously.

"Montana concern for chicken feed. Telegraphed the bank. Hurd got the cash before he shipped the horses. Foxy boy, Hurd. He made a deal with the Clespelems to help in future drives for him. Got the best of the other outfits."

"Yes, Blanding is rather crafty," his father had agreed dryly. "Ellery, you'd better let me invest your money, if it's any considerable amount."

"Dad, it's not enough for that," the young man had replied hastily. "Next drive I'll insist on fifty-fifty with Hurd."

Here Lark had been unable to contain herself longer. "You—you don't mean you've actually sold wild horses for chicken feed?"

"We sure have, cousin," he had replied, laughing. "And we're going to make a business of it."

"Monstrous!" Lark had burst out, and then had fled. But she did not get her door closed before she heard Ellery's remark to the others:

"That's odd. Do you suppose she cares?"

Lark had gone all over it in her mind, with the result that she wished she had kept silent. It was none of her business. They would never understand. But wild mustangs! Murdered for chicken feed! Was it not hideous? Chickens lived on corn and what they could scratch for. Whoever heard of feeding horseflesh to them? It was so utterly foreign to anything relating to horses or chickens as she knew them. The idea had been born in the fertile brain of some devilish cowboy. Hurd Blanding. Lark would remember that name.

Nothing could have been worse for Lark, upon the entrance to this new home, than to have heard of such brutality. She realized that her point of view was farfetched, and ridiculous to these town people. Most ranchers hated wild horses because they grazed on grass and drank up water which might have gone to sheep and cattle. Money was at the root of it.

In vain Lark tried to see the other side. But she did

understand that her feelings should not warp her against these relatives who had given her a home. She must not have such feelings, if that were possible. She was grateful and she meant to prove it. Nothing had been said to Lark about work, but she certainly would not be idle. She would earn her keep, if they would only allow her. Perhaps she could study something and earn money. And always in the back of her mind was the hope and the belief that she would someday return to Idaho.

Then she was confronted by an unforeseen contingency. The idea of going to the home of relatives to live had not greatly appealed to her, but neither had she felt fear or anxiety. Lark had taken it for granted that she would like, even love, the Wades. She had lived mostly in the country and worn jeans more than dresses. She had not had much schooling outside of her mother's teaching; still, there had not been any fear at the idea of mingling with more cultured people. She had not considered it much at all.

Here, however, confusing thoughts began to rise. Suppose she took a dislike to all the Wades, as she had to Ellery? What if she were taken for a country girl, a poor dependent cousin? She regarded these thoughts as selfish and unworthy of her. Nevertheless she realized, with a sinking of the heart, almost in dismay, that it was not going to be as she had dreamed it would be. She fortified herself against unknown things.

Lark's meditations were interrupted by a knock on her door. "Come—in," she faltered, wiping her eyes.

Marigold entered. She had changed her dress. Lark almost gasped. Marigold was a tall, perfect blonde, and the tight-fitting bodice of the full-skirted gown displayed her beautiful figure.

"May I come in and talk to you?" asked Marigold sweetly. She had light-blue languid eyes.

"I'd be glad to have you," replied Lark.

Whereupon her cousin sat down beside her. "I like this seat," she said. "It used to be mine—this room—before Dad fixed up the house. . . . Well, let's get acquainted."

"I'll do my best," replied Lark, smiling. Marigold

seemed friendly and kind. "First off, cousin, I'd like to know what's expected of me."

"Heavens! Nothing, except to make yourself at home."

"But I'll want some work."

"You might help Mother. And take care of your room. Lark, can you sew?"

"Yes, indeed."

"How're you fixed for clothes?"

"I've none to speak of, except this dress," returned Lark simply.

"You poor kid. Well, that's not much, old and faded. I've a lot of dresses I'll give you to make over, if you'll have them. And you'll need something new, too."

"You're very good, Marigold."

"We'll drive to town soon," said Marigold brightly. "You can buy some goods. Lark, what've you been used to down there in Idaho?"

"Ranch life. Work. Horses. Cattle."

"Any cowboys?"

"No. I have an old man who has been with us for years taking care of the place."

"Far from any town?"

"Yes. All-day ride for a horse."

"Any social life?"

"Not much. No neighbors. I've been to a few dances and weddings, christenings and such."

"Of course your town has a meeting house for dancing?"

"No. We used the schoolhouse. I have books too, but no late ones. We've been poor since my father died."

"Have you had fellows—beaux, I mean?"

"Sometimes, on Sundays. And not of my choice," rejoined Lark demurely.

"You've been really isolated. Lark, do you know you're not bad looking?"

"I hope I'm not."

"I'll bet when you're dressed you'll be a knockout. You'll need to change your hair—put it up."

"Cousin, my hair's unruly—and it's not very long anyhow."

"I see. It isn't so long at that. You can make it do.

You've lovely hair, Lark. I adore that ripple. And such a soft silky brown with red glints . . . El said you were good looking."

"Who's El?"

"My brother, Ellery. He's no good on earth. Only son, you know. Spoiled. Don't let him bother you, Lark. He imagines he's a devil with the women. But he's no good. We don't get along. Look out for El. He'll be after you, and I feel responsible for you, Lark. When Dad told us about you, and your situation down there, I persuaded him to send for you. You'll be a fleecy little lamb among wolves, I fear. But I don't want my brother to frighten you."

"Thank you, Marigold. But I can take care of myself," replied Lark with spirit, now that she thought she understood.

"Let me give you a hint about the rest of our family," went on Marigold. "Dad and Mom are blind about El. They think the sun rises and sets on him. They just can't see him as he is. So if he does get infatuated with you, it's not going to be easy. No girl is good enough for El, according to Mom. And Dad wants him settled. Dad has a big merchandise store in town. El hangs out there, where he's supposed to work. But outside of him, Dad and Mom are regular human beings, almost. Mom is easygoing, but Dad lets out a yell occasionally about money. That is when he's short of it. He sold a trainload of cattle lately and he's flush. So it'll be a good time for me to talk to him about going to town to shop. Let's go down and ask him right now."

Lark, thrilled and excited, though somewhat surprised at her cousin's point of view, tripped after Marigold downstairs. Mr. Wade was smoking in a chair, before a fire smoldering in the open grate. He was a well-preserved man, not much over fifty, with keen blue eyes and a tawny beard sprinkled with grey. It was plain where Marigold got her handsome features.

"Looks like a drive to me," he remarked quizzically, laying aside his paper. "Evidently you girls have got acquainted already."

"Give us time, Dad," replied Marigold. "Lark is not so easy to get acquainted with. She's lived pretty much alone down there on that ranch. I'd like to take her to town. She hasn't any clothes, naturally. May we go?"

"Reckon it's half a dozen for Lark an' six for you, eh?" he asked, laughing. "Sure you can go. Come here, Lark."

He appeared kindly and sympathetic, and as she stepped to his chair he took her hand and looked up with thoughtful, penetrating eyes. "Your father an' I were in the cattle business once, years ago, before you were born. He liked the unfenced ranges an' I leaned toward the settlements. I saw your mother once, just after her marriage. She was a dusky-eyed beauty. Indian blood, wasn't it?"

"My grandma was part Nez Percé, so Father used to say," replied Lark shyly.

"You favor your mother. Well, someday you must tell me all about yourself an' that ranch down in Idaho. You must try to fit in here an' make it home. I reckon it won't be easy at first."

"I'd like to work, Mr. Wade. Couldn't you give me work at your store?"

"Well!" Mr. Wade looked surprised. "It's not such a bad idea—if Mother an' Mari—"

"Mom wouldn't hear of it," interrupted Marigold.

"Daughter, there's nothin' like work an' independence," returned her father mildly. "Perhaps your cousin has been used to work. How about it, Lark?"

"I'm afraid I have," said Lark frankly, and she held out her hands. They were shapely, brown hands, but on the inside they were callused.

"Good heavens!" exclaimed Marigold.

"I see. Those hands haven't been idle," rejoined Mr. Wade, and Lark imagined his tone had added respect to its kindliness. "But, my dear, we can hardly let you do ranch work here."

"Can I have a horse?" asked Lark eagerly.

"I reckoned you liked horses, especially wild ones. Yes, you can take your pick."

"I love wild horses, Mr. Wade. I have caught them myself and broken them, too."

"All by yourself?" ejaculated Marigold incredulously.

"Yes. It's nothing to trap a wild pony. But it's a good deal to break him right."

"How old are you, Lark?"

"I'm not sure. I guess I'm going on nineteen."

"Nineteen and never had a beau?" asked Marigold flippantly. It might have been that she did not altogether like her father's sympathetic attitude.

"I'm sure about that last, cousin," returned Lark with just a note of aloofness.

"Lass, you an' I will get along," interposed the rancher. "Now you just settle yourself here an' make the best of it. Find some work, so you won't be too idle, as Mari is. Help around the house, read, an' ride all you want. I will talk with Mother about arrangin' an allowance for you."

"It's so wonderful—so good—of you," murmured Lark, feeling a birth of something warm and sweet in her. She liked the rancher's eyes. She sensed that all was not as he might have wanted it in that home.

"Dad, you are good," put in Marigold, kissing him. "We'll go to town tomorrow."

"All right, daughter. Get an early start, so you can be back early. It was past midnight last time."

"Remember, Dad, the buckboard broke a wheel," interrupted Marigold gaily. "I promise you not to be late. Come on, Lark. We'll run up to your room and make out a list.

"Say, Dad likes you," went on Marigold, when they were upstairs again. "He hasn't much use for flighty girls."

"I sure like him too," replied Lark fervently. "You don't know what it is to be without a father. Once I thought I'd never, never get over it."

"Say, child, what a shame. Haven't you had anybody to be fond of you?"

"No one, except my old farm hand, Jake."

"Lark, haven't you had a sweetheart? Honestly now?"

"I haven't, Marigold," protested Lark, with a blush. "I haven't. Cross my heart."

"Aren't there any cowboys in Idaho?"

"Yes, more than in Washington, I'd say. But none near my ranch. I met cowboys at the dances. I don't think much of cowboys. Last time there was a fight over me. So they said. I didn't see how it could be. But I avoided them after that."

"So you don't think much of cowboys," replied Marigold thoughtfully, with a speculative eye upon her cousin. "Neither do I. They're a conceited bunch. Stan doesn't like it when I look at one."

"Who's Stan?"

"Oh, he's my fiancé," said Marigold indifferently. "We've been engaged ever since I was sixteen. Before he went to college . . . Family affair. Well, Lark, my dear, let's make that list of what you need."

2

At noon the next day they arrived in the dusty town, which boasted a large merchandise store, several saloons, and a hotel and small restaurant. Lark was intrigued and delighted with the variety of materials and goods the store had to offer. Much more than she had ever seen before.

While they were examining and debating about the various colors and varieties of goods, Lark noticed, out of the corner of her eye, a masculine form emerge from the aisle.

"Here you are. I had a hard time finding you," someone said in a pleasant deep voice.

"Hello, Stan, I'm glad you rode over," replied Marigold. "Lark, I'd like you to meet my fiancé, Stanley Weston. Stan, my cousin, Lark Burrell, from Idaho. She has come to live with us."

"Miss Burrell, I'm happy to know you," replied Weston, with a slight bow.

"I'm happy to meet you, sir," Lark said shyly, gazing into serious dark eyes.

"Marigold, I have to see to my horse, but I'll meet you later and accompany you home," said Weston, turning to Marigold.

"That will be fine. We'll be ready at four."

Weston bowed again, and strode out.

A little before four, they were loading their purchases in the buckboard, with the help of the clerk, when Lark saw Marigold's fiancé. As he stepped out to meet the buckboard, lifting his hat, Lark sustained an unaccountable thrill. In the sunlight, bareheaded, he looked singularly pleasing. He was broad of shoulder and well above medium height.

He laughed. "Mari, you're on time for once."

"I don't want Dad to have reason to be angry. Look at all we've bought. Let's go," she said, gathering the reins as she stepped up into the buckboard.

The trip back was rapid—the horses were rested and anxious to get home. Marigold occupied herself with driving, while Weston questioned Lark about her life in Idaho. Lark found herself responding to his warm friendliness with ease, and was sorry when they arrived at the ranch.

That night dinner at the Wades' was another ordeal for Lark, though not so bad as that of the day before. Marigold was in high spirits, which Mr. Wade remarked was easy to understand. He was in good humor and asked Lark teasing questions. Ellery, who sat next to Lark, annoyed her by trying to get hold of her hand. But it was the thought of Stanley which made the dinner much too long for the girl.

After dinner the goods, both Lark's and Marigold's, had to be shown for Mrs. Wade's edification. She was as pleased as the girls. Indeed, Marigold had a faithful ally in her mother.

"But, dear, it seems such useless extravagance—I mean your purchases—when you will be getting married soon, surely this fall," remarked her mother.

Marigold flushed red, and it was evident to Lark that

she saw red too. "Mother, I've *told* you I don't want to get married soon," she retorted.

"You should. You're twenty-two."

"Suppose I am? That's not old—it's young. I don't want to settle down and have children and be old before I know it. I'm having a good time. Besides, Stan wants me to live in that old ranch house of his, with his old father. I want to live in town. We're argued about it often. I wish you'd let me alone. It just upsets me. I'll do as I please, anyhow."

"So we have observed," retorted Mrs. Wade, with resignation. "But Marigold, you should realize things as they are. We are not rich, by any means. Your father has sold out. That money, most of it, must go to pay debts and put his store in better shape to meet competition. Now Stanley Weston is, or will be, a wealthy man. Take care you don't play around so long that you'll lose him."

"Oh!" cried Marigold, furiously, as her mother left the room. "Lark, I sure have trouble with my parents. You don't know when you're well off. Dad isn't so bad, except when he's worried about money. But Mother makes me sick. If she isn't nagging me for riding or dancing, she's nagging me to marry Stan."

"Marigold, it's only that she's so anxious to see you settled for life," replied Lark sympathetically.

"That's right! That's just it," replied the girl passionately. "Well, I'm rot ready to be settled."

"I should think you'd be eager—to marry Mr. Weston," ventured Lark.

"Oh, I like Stan well enough. But we never get along. He doesn't approve of me, Lark."

"He seemed very nice. Of course, I don't know any young men."

"Your good fortune is about at an end," retorted Marigold sarcastically. "There'll be a flock of them after you presently, including El. Mother will be keen to marry you to one—*not* El, but the one who has the best prospects."

"Me! Marry? Oh, how funny!" exclaimed Lark, half in mirth and half in consternation.

"It *is* funny, to see it our way. But look at it with *their* eyes. The old women are always matchmaking. You're a female, young, healthy, pretty, and poor as a church mouse. They'd have you baking, sewing, scrubbing—and nursing kids for some man."

"That last is fearful to think of," agreed Lark, laughing in spite of her shocked sensibilities. "At least for you. But it seems sort of—out of the question for me."

"Ha ha! You'll see."

A deep pleasant voice called up the stairs: "Mari, I'd like to see you a minute before I leave."

"I'll come down, Stan," called Marigold in reply, as she rose, and smoothed her skirt and left the room.

Presently another voice made itself heard. "Sis, where's Lark?"

"She's in her room. And she's tired. It's been some day for her," Lark heard Marigold reply.

"Hey, Lark," Ellery called, still louder.

"Yes, what is it?" rejoined Lark, going to the door somewhat perturbed. But she might as well meet this situation.

"Come to the head of the stairs."

Lark went, and, leaning over the rail, saw the young man looking up.

"Let's go for a ride," he proposed eagerly.

"Ride! I've had enough rides—for today."

"Let's go out and walk then."

Lark wanted to walk outdoors, but there was no temptation in going with Ellery. She did not care to go with him, anywhere.

"Thanks, Mr. Wade, but I'm tired."

"Say, don't be so formal. Call me El. . . . Well, what do you know about that?"

Lark had gone back toward her room. She heard Marigold say: "I told you to leave Lark alone, El. She's not for you."

"What's that talk?" spoke up Mrs. Wade curiously.

"Aw, Sis is ragging me for asking Lark to go riding."

"Why should you do that, Marigold?" returned the mother.

"Mom, Lark doesn't want to go out with El. She said so."

"Oh, indeed. I should think she'd be glad—and proud to go," returned Mrs. Wade stiffly.

"Well, you're wrong, Mother darling."

Lark, who had hesitated and then stopped in the hallway, hurried to her room and closed the door. She sat down, staring blankly at the purchases spread on her bed.

She thought of her conversation with Stanley, on the way home—how kind he was—and she became conscious of a vague, sweetly stirring, infinitely remote sensation of warmth—of pleasure. It was the way he looked at her when she was telling of breaking colts and riding along the Salmon River. It had to do with his nearness to her, when her unruly hair blew across his face. She found that she liked both those incidents, and felt uneasiness that this should be so.

After Lark's first flush of consternation she straightened out the matter in her mind. She had known confusing things would happen to her in this new home. She would be lifted to the sky and then cast down. She would be puzzled, perplexed, upset, furious, unhappy. She would be jealous, envious, miserable, all because she was a girl and could not help it. She was bound to be pleased by Marigold's family and friends, and also displeased. Mr. Stanley Weston, her cousin's fiancé, had pleased her, that was all, and Lark decided gravely to try to forget it.

3

NEXT MORNING Lark waited to be called to breakfast. She was usually up with the bird for which her father had named her. It seemed a long while until the breakfast hour, but at last she heard a bell. She encountered Marigold in a bright blue gown, which enhanced her blonde beauty.

"Hello, Lark. I forgot to tell you about breakfast hour," she said. "It's any time. Dad and El leave early for the store. Mom is seldom down and I never am. Cookie will give you eats any time."

"Seems like I've been up hours," rejoined Lark. "I didn't sleep very well. Heard horses more than once."

"Let's go down. . . . Stan left last night in a rage. I went to town. Didn't get back till late."

They had breakfast alone, to Lark's relief.

"Say, Lark, for heaven's sake, throw away that gray dress, will you? It looks dreadful."

"All right, I will—after this time. Marigold, can I see the horses and ride this morning?"

"Of course. Maybe I'll go with you. What have I got to do, anyway? No, I can't. . . . But you don't need me. Put on your riding clothes and go out to the barn. Hurd won't be there—he was drunk last night. . . . But some of the boys will be there. Tell them I said you could have any horse in the outfit. So you take your pick."

"Oh, thank you, cousin. That will be grand," cried Lark, thrilled at the prospect. "And where will I ride?"

"There's a thousand miles of sage back of the ranch, more or less," laughed Marigold. "Lark, I'm glad *that* makes you look happy. We've got horses and sage enough, Lord knows. And do I need to warn you against cowboys?"

"Hardly. I reckon cowboys are all alike."

"They are, and no good on earth, except—well, so long, Lark. Don't ride clear to Horse Heaven Hill."

Lark ran upstairs and soon, in a delight that caused her a mild astonishment, she had donned her riding garb. She laughed at her image in the big mirror. She was a boy once more, in jeans, boots, spurs, blouse and all, even to a battered old sombrero, which she pulled down over her wavy locks. Then, gloves in hand, she went sideways down the stairs, careful not to tear the carpet with her long spurs, and slipping out the back way, much to Cookie's amazement, she took the path that led to the barns.

She had seen them from a distance, and now, nearing them, she was to learn what a big ranch meant, in barns and corrals, sheds and cribs, with wide green pastures beyond, spotted with horses. For the first moment since Lark had left home she felt natural, sure of herself, and really happy. She did not show in the least her elation and surprise at the sight of a Western ranch. She reveled in the well-loved sounds and smells.

The main barn was a huge affair, with a wide lane through the center and numerous stalls on each side. A slanting runway led up to the level of the floor. Three cowboys were sitting there, indulging in some game. They wore the customary garb of riders, rough and worn, yet they did not, upon closer view, appear as tough as the cowboys around Batchford.

"Howdy, sonny, what you want?" asked one of them casually, after a glance at her.

"I want a horse," replied Lark.

"You don't say?" returned the rider, as he bent over the dice his companion was throwing. "What for do you want a horse?"

"To ride."

"Got any dough?"

"Dough?—No, I haven't."

"Well, beat it then," he said, snatching at the dice.

Lark sat down across the wide entrance, in such a way that she aided the deception she had begun unwittingly and now began to revel in. She watched them awhile unmolested, as evidently her interrogator had forgotten her. They threw dice, complained, swore mildly. The one who had spoken was bareheaded, a young fellow, clean-cut and smooth-faced, very nice-looking indeed. The second was redheaded and somewhat coarse. The third was older, in his late twenties, which meant maturity for a cowboy. He had strikingly handsome features. His eyes were cast down. There were blue circles under them. His lips and chin were boldly chiseled.

"Damn you, Hurd. Lucky in dice as lucky in women!" complained the cowboy next to him.

"It's not luck; I'm smart," replied the other, spreading the dice.

Here Lark pricked up her ears, even more interested. This one must be Hurd Blanding, the cowboy associated with Ellery Wade in the wild-horse drive. Marigold, too, had mentioned him.

"You won't be smart at all if Stan Weston gets wise to you," came the significant reply. Whereupon Blanding flung the dice at the other.

"Shut up. If you make another crack like that I'll—"

He noticed Lark then and checked his speech. He had wonderful, hard, light eyes.

"Who the hell is this, Coil?" he asked, nudging the bareheaded cowboy, and indicating Lark.

"Some kid who came in here asking for a horse . . . Hey, didn't I tell you to beat it?"

"Reckon you did," replied Lark, almost giggling, as she sat, elbows on her knees, her hands at the flap of her sombrero. How she wished that the innocent deceit could be prolonged!

Blanding searched around with eye and hand, manifestly for something to throw at Lark. At that moment his look justified her intuition—he had an evil face, undeniably handsome though it was. He found a piece of wood, which he flung at Lark, accompanying the action with a harsh: "Get out!" The missile struck Lark on her right foot; a glancing blow, but it hurt. She stood up.

"My cousin Marigold sure has a fine lot of cowboys," she said contemptuously.

Lark's movement and change of tone were followed by a blank silence. Not until she stepped out where they could see her plainly did they accept her sex. Blanding was the first to recover. He rose to his superb height and doffed his sombrero.

"Miss, you can lay it to your ridin' outfit," he said, with a winning smile. "We wanted to give you a little fun, seein' you looked like a boy. But I knew you all the time."

The other cowboys leaped up, and, not to be outdone,

the clean-cut youth, called Coil by his companions, stepped out.

"I'm sure awful sorry, Miss Burrell," he apologized. And the redheaded fellow nodded and grinned sheepishly, as if to stand by his comrade,

"You're all liars," replied Lark coolly. "You didn't know me from Adam."

"Well, Red an' I didn't throw clubs at you, anyway," returned Coil significantly.

"It was only in fun, Miss Lark," protested Hurd, not in the least concerned. "And it didn't hit you."

"Like fun it didn't," retorted Lark indignantly. "It almost crippled me." And she exaggerated a limp.

"Maybe you're not as tough as you look," remarked Blanding facetiously. "That outfit has had more than one bump, I'll bet."

Lark had to acknowledge to herself that Blanding had keen eyes. She did not care much for the look in them.

"Do I get a horse or must I go back to tell Marigold that I was insulted?"

"Aw, Miss Burrell, don't be too hard on me an' Red, anyway," asked Coil appealingly. "I apologize for my part. Miss Wade would sure fire *us*."

The emphasis on the us, which significantly eliminated Blanding, was not lost upon Lark. There was something here, almost dismaying, that stimulated her thought.

"In your case, then, I'll believe you were only in fun," replied Lark kindly.

"Thanks, miss. You can ride any horse," began Coil, beaming, but Blanding thrust him and Red back.

"I'm boss here. Now, Miss Lark, what kind of a horse do you want?"

"Any kind that will go," rejoined Lark slowly, as the two disgruntled cowboys walked out of the barn. Coil looked back at Blanding, a scowl marring his youthful face.

"Can you ride?" asked Blanding in a flattering tone. He stepped close to her, looking down. He was a superb animal and knew it.

"Oh, yes, tolerable."

"You look like a cowgirl. I'll bet you've ridden at rodeos."

"No. I've just been a ranch hand."

"Come here. Take a peep at Mari—Miss Wade's horse," said Blanding, and he circled his fingers around Lark's elbow, leading her to a stall. It might have been nothing, this action, and then again it might have been a good deal. He kept his hand there while he showed Lark her cousin's favorite, a dark bay mare with white feet. They went on to the next stall, and the next, down the line on that side of the stable. Lark had been used all her life to good horses. These fine animals of Mr. Wade's scarcely needed Blanding's eloquence. He wanted to talk. He wanted to impress Lark.

Across the aisle in the first stall a white-faced horse poked his head over the bars and whinnied. He took Lark's eye.

"This here is Chaps," went on Blanding. "He's from Oregon, an' I'll say they sure raise horseflesh in that state."

"They're all wonderful," burst out Lark in delight. "Saddle Chaps for me."

"I knew he'd be the one. You're a swell picker, Miss Lark. . . . An' you're goin' to let me ride with you?" He squeezed her arm and drew her so that she rested against him, and gazed down upon her in a bold and masterful way. It was new to Lark, though she had been importuned by cowboys, and it both excited and repelled her. But remembering Marigold's hint, Lark kept her wits about her. "I reckon I got to see what you look like," he went on coolly, and removed her sombrero.

"Do I look like a boy now?" asked Lark.

"Say, girl, it's downright cruel an' mean to hide your hair an' face," he exploded, bending lower. "Under a deceivin' old slouch hat like this."

"Why so?" rejoined Lark provocatively.

"Because you're most awful pretty."

"Thank you. But that's nothing. Give me my old slouch hat."

Manifestly, Blanding did not require much time or opportunity to make advances toward a girl. Lark, owing to some vague subtle connection between her cousin and this cowboy which she had grasped, had not reacted immediately upon her instincts. Probably her apparent laxity had deceived him; more probably Blanding was not the kind of man to need encouragement. But when he deliberately bent lower, his face heating, she was sure of her suspicions and thrust him away with no light hand. Then she snatched her sombrero.

"Keep your paws off me, cowboy," she said, in a tone only a conceited fool could have misunderstood.

"Wha-what?" he stammered, very certainly surprised.

"That's what I said. Mr. Blanding, it doesn't follow because you can get fresh with these girls around here that you can do it with a little country jake from down Idaho."

Lark learned more from his suddenly flaming face than from any other circumstance that had occurred.

"Say, has Marigold been shootin' off her chin to you?" he demanded, recovering. That question defined his status, as well as gave Lark a most decided concern. Could it be possible— She quelled the thought.

"No. My cousin did not mention you, if that is what you meant," she replied haughtily.

"Oh . . . Well, I—you—it sure sounded as if somebody had put you against me," he floundered, seeking a way out. He had no sense of shame.

"It wasn't necessary. Any decent girl could figure you out in five minutes. Less time if she was alone with you!"

"Say, Lark—"

"What right have you to call me Lark?" she interrupted. "I'm Miss Burrell to you, or any other cowboy."

"All right, Miss Burrell," he said, forced to recognize something astounding. "But I didn't mean any harm. I—"

"No, you didn't," retorted Lark scornfully. "You're a fine gentlemanly cowboy! You threw a club at me—"

"I didn't know you were a girl."

"There! I've caught you in a lie. . . . You threw a club at me and two minutes afterward you'd have kissed me."

"What's a kiss, anyway?" he asked, in a conciliatory tone.

"It's a great deal to some girls."

"Maybe so, but I don't believe it."

"Well, it's an insult to me anyhow. I—shall tell Marigold."

This was an unconsidered random shot that found its mark. For the first time consternation and alarm appeared in his mobile face.

"Please, Miss Burrell, don't do that," he begged, suddenly sincere. And sincerity made him appealing. "Can't you make allowance? You've a most awful pretty face. Red lips! . . . Seein' them sudden like, without any warnin'—I—I lost my head. I get fool notions over girls. Maybe this was love at first sight."

"Maybe it wasn't," drawled Lark, enjoying Blanding's right-about-face.

"Don't you believe in love at first sight?"

"Sure, in the case of cowboys with any girl. But Mr. Blanding, I want a horse. I can't stay here all day listening to you."

"But please don't tell her. She'd fire me."

"I daresay that would be a calamity for Wade Ranch, in your opinion."

"For me it would. You won't tell her?"

"Unless I change my mind I certainly will," returned Lark vehemently. "You're not doing your cause any good by this talk. What kind of a man are you, anyway? I'm used to cowboys who do what they're told to do. This is a funny kind of ranch."

Lark felt that she was stretching the truth a bit, as far as her experience went, but it was logical. She saw that she had finally subdued Blanding. He led the horse out of the stall. Then Lark quite forgot everything else. Chaps was a beauty, a cream-colored mustang with white markings, and if he did not have a strain of wild blood, she was greatly mistaken. Evidently he did not like Blanding.

"Let me have him. You get a bridle and saddle. . . . Here, Chaps. That's a poor name for you. Whoa now, White-face. I'll call you that, or better—Cream Puff."

It did not take a moment for Lark to make up with him. A horse that is spirited, and nervous with men, very often is easy to handle by women. Chaps had never been hurt by a woman.

"You sure have a way with horses," remarked Blanding as he returned.

"Yes. But it's not like yours with ladies, Mr. Blanding. . . . Thanks, but I'll bridle him."

Lark put the bridle on, then the blankets, which she smoothed and patted out. The saddle was not a light one by any means, but she swung it up with one hand, easily and sweepingly, in a manner to make the watching cowboy whistle.

"I hate a single cinch, but reckon—" she said, speaking to herself.

"We haven't a double-cinch saddle on the ranch," Blanding informed her.

Lark made no reply. The cowboy had ceased to exist for her just then. She pulled the cinch, lightly at first, watching the mustang, and then she tightened it. That done, she put on gloves and sombrero, which she had laid aside.

"Reckon the stirrups will be about right," vouchsafed Blanding. "They have been lengthened since one of Miss Wade's girl friends rode here last week."

Lark measured them with her arm. Then gathering up the reins she grasped the pommel with both hands. Up she vaulted into the saddle, without ever touching the stirrup.

"Get out of here, Cream Puff," Lark called gaily, and she was off. The barnyard gate stood ajar, and down the lane another gate was open, and two cowboys, probably the ones Blanding had driven off, stood by waiting. Lark touched the mustang with the spurs. He broke from a trot into a gallop. The cowboys waved their hats.

Lark found herself beyond the fences, out on an old sandy road, with the open sage ahead. She could have screamed her joy. On a horse again! The purple reaches calling! She asked no more. She left her problems behind and raced for the sage.

4

Stanley Weston lived alone with his father, an invalid during his later years. He had been one of the pioneer settlers of that section of Washington, having traveled there from Pennsylvania as a young man.

It was no wonder that the old man loved Sage Hill Ranch and that his great hope was for Stanley to carry on there. The location was beautiful, besides having many associations dear to the pioneer. The ranch house stood on a gradually rising bench of sage, which spread out from an eminence called Sage Hill. There was more pine on it than sage. The massive logs of which the house was built had come off that hill. A number of springs united to form a fine brook of cold, clear water, which was no small item in the value of the immense ranch. Weston had in the early days acquired thousands of acres which were now valuable. He owned fine standing timber; there were hundreds of horses on the thousand-acre pasture which he had fenced; and there was no end of cattle. Weston also owned wheat farms south of Wadestown.

Stanley rode home early from Wadestown that night. An argument with Marigold, not the first by any means, had left him more than usually pensive and sad. Such moods had been more frequent of late. He had taken Marigold to task, and not for the first time, about something he believed she should not have done and they quarreled. Never again, he vowed! Then his thoughts turned to Marigold's cousin, the girl from south Idaho who called herself Lark. "Name somehow suits her," he thought.

The air was cold and brisk. He slowed up a bit, so that the wind would not be so piercing. Sage Hill loomed dark against the star-fired sky. On each side of the road spread the almost flat land, dim and monotonous, spectral under the stars, and redolent with sage.

Soon Stanley reached the winding road between the low foothills, from which it was only a short distance up the slope to the ranch house.

The hour was still early enough for his father to be in the living room, his hands spread to a bright fire. He had a fine shaggy head and a gray rugged face. It was easy to see where Stanley got his stature.

"Wal howdy, son, reckon I didn't expect you home tonight," the rancher greeted Stanley as he breezed in.

"Glad to get home, believe me," returned Stanley, eager to get near the fire. "It was cold. I met Marigold in town. She had a cousin with her, a girl named Burrell from Idaho. I rode back with them."

"Burrell. I remember him. Pardner of Wade's years ago. Real Westerner of the old school. Married a part-Indian girl. What was the girl like?"

"Pretty. Shy. Strange—after these girls. She won't last long at Wade's."

"Ahuh. How'd it come aboot thet she's there?"

"Well, I gathered that she was an orphan, living on a rundown ranch, on the Salmon River in Idaho. Do you know that country, Dad?"

"Grand country, son. Wild yet, I reckon."

"I'd like to see it. . . . The Wades offered her a home and here she is. That's all I know."

"Is she like these heah town lasses?" asked Weston shortly.

"How do you mean, Dad?" inquired Stanley, his eyes twinkling.

"Wal, aboot the flirtin'—leadin' the boys on an' so forth?"

Stanley laughed heartily at his father. The modern young woman was one of the incomprehensible things to the older man's generation. They were not out of accord on the subject, though Stanley, being a college graduate, sought to preserve a broad, liberal mind.

"No, Dad. Lark is not in the least like 'these here town lasses.' I wonder—"

"Lark? Thet her name?"

"Yes. I couldn't tell you just why, but it suits her."

"Sight better'n Marigold. Thet's a hell of a name," growled Weston. "Suppose you fetch Lark up to see me. I get lonesome oftener than I used to. Mebbe we'd hit it off. I'd like to know somethin' aboot thet Salmon country."

"Dad, I'll be glad to," spoke up Stanley, surprised. "Bet she'd like to come. . . . It's a long time, though, Dad, since you asked to see Marigold."

Stanley spoke with unconscious wistfulness, and half to himself. The old man was silent. He turned round before the fire. Stanley sighed.

"Dad, you don't approve of Marigold. Oh, I know, and it worries me."

"Wal, son, do you approve of her?" inquired the rancher, in his blunt way.

The query shocked Stanley and brought a recurrence of the mood in which he had not long since left Marigold.

"Dad, a fellow must certainly approve of the girl he's going to marry."

"Ahuh. I reckon so, an' make himself blind to do it."

"Dad, let's have it out. Let's lay the cards on the table. . . . Gradually you have lost something for Marigold. You used to love her."

The rancher pulled his chair closer to the fire, opening his big hands to the warmth, as was his habit.

"Put a couple of chunks on, Stan. . . . Shore, I used to love Mari. Before you went to college an' she growed up. Mother was livin' then. She was fond of Mari. But all seems changed, son. I don't say Mari isn't lovable yet. She is. But, if you must know, I can't stand the change in her lately."

"What do you mean, Dad?" questioned Stanley gravely.

"Wal, you know, son, I reckon."

"Yes, I know, but do you?"

"Son, I can see what the girl has on her mind, which is not much these days. I can see how she acts an' I can heah what she says—an' what's said aboot her."

"You've heard gossip about Marigold?"

"Reckon I have, son."

"Those gabby old women friends of yours! . . . Dad, I don't want to get sore. But they don't understand Marigold and neither do you. How often have I tried to make you see! Times are changing. More women go to college and become more independent."

Stanley spoke with earnest passion and he anticipated a pondering wait for an answer. But it came like a flash.

"Stan," the rancher said, "my advice to you is marry her just as quick as ever you can. Wifehood and motherhood have been natural to women for a long time. This heah foolin' around hasn't been. An' it's takin' a risk. I'm not blamin' the girls, Stan. I'm blamin' the times. An' if I was you I'd put a halter on Mari."

"Dad, I must confess to you," returned Stanley shamefacedly, "I—I quarreled with Marigold tonight over that very thing. I wanted her to marry me in June. She refused —said she could not possibly get ready before June a year. I argued with her, tried to persuade her. No go! She wants her freedom for a while. That riled me, of course. We had it out hot and heavy. And I beat it home before the storm subsided."

"Ahuh. Wal, what're you goin' to do aboot it?"

"I don't know, Dad."

"Humph. Do you still love Mari?"

"Love her!—Why, I never thought of anything different," replied Stanley, aghast at the thought. It puzzled him, too.

"Love changes, son. An' it doesn't last forever, in some cases. I can't see that Mari loves you heaps. If she did, she wouldn't set such store on this precious freedom. She'd want you. She'd want to come out heah pronto, an' give a woman's touch to this old home once more, an' see thet there were children around heah before I die."

"Lord help me, Dad, you're right! I've thought that, only I just wouldn't believe it. What can I do?"

"Wal, I'm glad you asked thet," responded the old man. "We've been close together, father an' son, as blood ties go these days. When I sent you to college I was afraid you'd get a leanin' toward the cities an' mebbe prefer them. But you didn't. You care for the old ranch. It's shore made me happy. I couldn't ask no more, unless for you to fetch a wife home."

"Dad, I've been happy, too, until lately," rejoined Stanley, just as earnestly. "I love the open country. City life would never suit me. There's a big development to work out on this ranch. But for weeks I've been at a standstill. No use lying. It's on account of Marigold."

"Ahuh. A woman can shore raise hell with a man," replied his father grimly, nodding his shaggy head. "Listen, son. It may be hard for you to see, but it's not for me. . . . If you feel thet Mari is honest an' true, give her the benefit of a doubt an' more time. Be good to her. No naggin' or fightin'."

"Thanks, Dad. I'll think it over," responded Stanley soberly.

"Don't waste no more time, Stan. Life is short. . . . Reckon I'll go to bed now. I'm glad you confided in me. Good night, son."

Stanley sat there long after his father left, and until the fire burned down to a bed of glowing coals. The wind moaned outside and the coyotes howled. In this lonely hour Stanley thought he had made an end of indecision, of hoping against hope.

Next morning, after breakfast, Stanley rode down away from the ranch toward the foothills to the west. He had donned his old riding outfit, and he rode his favorite horse. The spring morning was gloriously bright, cool, crisp; the sky shone bright blue; the wind off the sage brought a sweet, thick fragrance, always so strong and welcome.

Once down on the winding trail he put Boots to a long swinging lope toward an isolated foothill, round and beautiful, banded with gray sage halfway up and then covered with pines. It stood about an equal distance from Sage Hill and Wadestown, approximately ten miles.

In the course of an hour or more Stanley reached the edge of the gradual slope, where he reined Boots to a walk. His habit was to ride up to the pines, tie his horse there, and with his field glasses study the range.

This intention, however, was frustrated by a rider coming down the trail from the direction Stanley was bent upon. He saw that he had been noticed as quickly as his keen eyes had sighted a horse. The rider had just come around the slope and looked like a bareheaded boy, mounted on Marigold's cream-colored mustang. Stanley thought that was strange, for Marigold certainly would not let any boy use that horse. Perhaps Hurd Blanding was responsible.

The rider looked, halted, then, jamming on a sombrero, wheeled the mustang as if to depart hurriedly. The distance was more than a hundred yards, but Stanley recognized that shining, curly head before it was covered.

"Hold on, Lark!" he called piercingly.

That stopped her, whereupon Stanley, spurring Boots, quickly covered the intervening distance.

"Well, of all things, Lark Burrell, way out here in the sage!" exclaimed Stanley, in surprise and pleasure. His swift glance took her in from the battered old sombrero to her top boots and long spurs. She looked the real thing.

"Good morning, Mr. Weston," she replied.

"Didn't you recognize me? You were going to beat it."

"Yes, I—I'm ashamed to say I knew you and was going to run."

"Why, for goodness' sake?"

"I was sure you wouldn't know me—in this rig. . . . And I—well—fact is, I haven't any good excuse, except I was scared."

"You had a right to be," he returned seriously. "You shouldn't ride way out here alone. There are Indians and outlaws back in those hills. It's just as well, too, for you not to meet some of our cowboys."

"Shucks. They couldn't catch me."

"Chaps is fast, all right. But can you ride?"

"A little," she replied, leaning over, the better to see all around Stanley's horse. Then she sat up, eager and excited. "Oh, that's a horse you're on. Can he run?"

"Rather. Best on the range."

"Is he? Bet he couldn't catch me."

"I'll bet you he could. Want to try?"

"No. But he couldn't. You are too heavy."

Stanley conceded the point without argument. Evidently this girl from southern Idaho understood horses. With what ease and grace she sat her saddle! She was as lithe as an Indian. Stanley's eyes made note of the service her rider's outfit had evidently rendered. His glance, however, quickly traveled back to her face, only partly hidden under the limp, wide flap of the old sombrero. Stanley had seen her before, and bareheaded, too, but somewhere she was marvelously different today.

"What are you doing way out here?" he asked.

"Riding. Seeing your country. Oh, it's glorious. I'm afraid I'm drunk on sage. We have sage down in Idaho, but not like this. Not blue and thick!"

"You like my sage country then?"

"I love it. I had no idea it was so beautiful—so sweet. Marigold never said a word about the sage or the hills or, well, anything except I'd get a thrill out of town, anyway."

"Did you?"

"Not one thrill. Not one, Mr. Weston, and it worries me," she replied.

"How about the pretty dresses?"

"Oh, they had some effect on me. No thrill though. Should they?"

"Some girls think so. I just had a very pleasant one—when I came around the slope to see you. I'm afraid my mood was rather gloomy."

The remark brought back her shyness, and he regretted it. He would have to be sincere with this girl. A tinge of red slowly receded from the gold-brown cheek.

"By the way, where is Marigold?" he asked, getting back to sterner reality, which he certainly was reluctant to do.

"Home. She said she'd come. But she didn't. She was out late last night."

Stanley gazed away across the sage. So Marigold went, after all! A little fire ran along his veins. Presently he turned again to the girl, to observe that instantly she averted her eyes.

"Chaps is pretty warm. Why not rest him?"

"Yes, I was about to walk him when you came in sight. . . . His name is not Chaps for me, but Cream Puff."

"Good. I like yours better," commended Stanley, but did not divulge that the reason was that Blanding had named the mustang.

"What's the name of yours?" asked Lark, reaching a guarded hand to his horse.

"Boots."

"The same as Marigold calls you? Very poorly named, both of you."

"Boots harks back to my football days at the university."

"Football.. There's so much I've never seen," said the girl dreamily. "When were you in college?"

"I graduated in June, two years ago."

"Did Marigold ever see you play?"

"Oh, yes, often." Then abruptly changing the subject, he said, "Lark, let's get off and rest ourselves, while your horse is resting."

"Really I—I ought to start back," she rejoined, but it was certain that she seemed impelled to stay.

"Come. It's hours till lunchtime. And what's the difference, anyhow?" he urged, seriously enough.

"All right," she agreed, and swinging her leg she slipped off in a single movement. Then standing there, she seemed different again, taller, slimmer, yet undeniably a girl.

Stanley dismounted, and taking the reins of her horse he suggested, "Let's go up to the pines. It's only a step or so. You'll like the view."

It was more than a step, but she followed him without comment. Soon they reached the band of pines, growing far apart, black and straight, with their spreading branches of thin foliage rustling in the wind. The ground was brown with pine needles.

"It's pleasant here—if you have no hounding memories," said Stanley, smiling at her, as she stood uncertain and shy before him, bareheaded again. How rich and thick her brown hair was with its glints of gold! In the clear open light he saw her eyes to better advantage than at any time before—dark, velvety eyes, full of tawny, slumberous depths. They did not meet his.

"Sit here, Lark, and look out across the sage toward Horse Heaven Hill. Isn't that the limit of a name? I'll get my field glasses."

He returned presently to find Lark absorbed in the view. It pleased him that she seemed rapt. Once upon a time Marigold, sitting right there, had lain back on the pine needles to laugh at his rhapsodies on the scenery, and she had drawled, "Ain't nature grand?" He had never let himself go again, regarding the beauty of anything. Remembering, he was curious to see how this girl would respond. He waited a long while, during which he did not yield to his desire to look at her instead of the expanse before them.

Still, the scene was always soul-satisfying to Stanley, somehow unaccountably tranquilizing and helpful. He needed it now. The wind was out of the west and had just lost its cool edge, but appeared more laden with the incense of the sage. The slope below them slanted away gradually, down to the level expanse, which extended westward in fifty miles of unbroken plain, rolling in leagues of slow ascent or descent onto the blue mountain that was called a haven for wild horses.

"Oh, so lovely!" murmured the girl at last. "All so gray, so lonely, so monotonous!"

"Lark, you have hit upon its fascination," replied Stanley gladly. "The endless gray, the loneliness, the eternal monotony!—Oh, you have not disappointed me."

She flashed at him a fleeting, surprised look, enough to make him marvel at what her eyes might express if they were given a cue to love or passion. She had depth, this girl, and feeling.

"I see wild horses out there," she said.

"You do? Where? I can't see any. You must have the eye of an eagle."

"I might be wrong. Let me have your glasses."

While she adjusted these and trained them on the gray expanse, Stanley bent his own unsatisfied gaze upon the curly, shapely head, the clear, tanned cheek, the rounded neck and shoulder, the strong brown wrists and hands. She was astoundingly attractive.

"Yes, I thought so. Wild horses! And sure a lot of them."

"Lark, you love wild horses," he asserted, not asking.

"More than anything. My country is full of them. Oh, how I wish those wild horses out there could get down to the ranges of the Salmon! Then they would be free."

"I'm with you, Lark. You've heard of the drive made recently. Hurd Blanding and El Wade pulled it off. Bribed the Clespelems. It stuck in my craw, that deal. Three dollars a head—for chicken feed!"

"Oh, it was hideous!" cried Lark, in sudden low passion. "All for a little money! Those wild horses are not grazing off the range. There's ten times as much feed here as we have in Idaho."

"Pretty raw, I'll agree, Lark," rejoined Stanley. "There were some good ponies in that wild bunch. I saw them. Made me sick—the way they had them tailed."

"Tailed! What's that?" asked Lark swiftly, and now he almost jumped under the full gaze of her eyes, wonderful, clear, almost hard.

"The cowboys call it tailing. It's done after they trap the horses."

"They lasso them, throw them, and tie the tail of one to the head of another?"

"Precisely. And it's rotten, believe me."

"I feared that. I've heard of it. Oh, I hate them—I hate them! If any cowpunchers did that on my range I'd shoot them."

Stanley realized then, with the bell-like ring of her voice in his ear, that he had passed the stage of interest in Lark Burrell. He was wholly fascinated. Lying back upon the pine needles, he closed his eyes and tried to think.

★

5

"Please say, Mr. Weston, that—you'll persuade Marigold to influence her brother and that Blanding cowboy not to drive wild horses again," begged the girl.

Stanley sat up and opened his eyes. He felt he ought to use them without trying to think.

"I'll do that little thing, Lark, but I fear it's useless."

"Thank you. Oh, I know I'm queer to you folks up here, Mr. Weston—"

"Stop saying 'mister,' won't you, Lark? Call me Stan, or Stanley. But not Boots. Will you?"

"Why yes, of course, if you want—and Marigold doesn't mind," she returned shyly.

Stanley laughed loud and not without a little bitterness. "Child, what do you say to this? My fiancée calls other men—old friends—such names as darling and sweetheart. Of course, that doesn't mean anything, but—"

"I—I didn't mean anything."

"Enough said. Never you mind about Marigold."

"I'm afraid I can't help minding. I haven't known any engaged couples. But—but you two are all—all—"

"All wrong, Lark. You said it," he began earnestly. "But listen. We've been engaged for over five years. College changed Marigold. Maybe it changed me, but I can't *see* it. . . . Thank God, I can be honest with one girl."

He had his reward in a lovely, startled face that was at once averted from his burning gaze.

"Don't be upset, Lark," he went on composedly. "I just wanted you to know that things aren't just right between Marigold and me."

"But she—she loves you," returned Lark solemnly.

"How do you know? Did she say so?"

"Oh, no, she told me very little. But she *must*."

"Why?" asked Stanley laconically.

Evidently this was a knotty question for Lark. "Because you're engaged and—and everything."

"My young friend from the Salmon River—listen. Being engaged doesn't seem to affect Marigold at all. She—"

Stanley thought he had better check his impetuosity. But what a relief it would be to unburden himself!

"You're just angry with Marigold," went on Lark gently. "And you know how it is when one is that way. Marigold is a gay, happy, thoughtless, beautiful girl. You are very lucky, Stanley. She *must* love you."

"All right. Maybe. Anyway, you're good to champion her," replied Stanley, forcing his mind off Marigold. "Tell me about yourself. Of course you have a sweetheart. Girls who live in the sticks always do."

"Oh dear no! And what do you mean by 'sticks'? It doesn't sound nice."

"I mean the backwoods. Lark, don't try any south Idaho line with me. That is to say—don't lie. This is a very serious occasion. You have a beau?"

"No, Stanley, I've never had even an admirer that Dad would let come to see me—or I would have seen after Dad was gone."

"What's the matter with the fellows down there?" asked Stanley incredulously.

"There aren't any. Oh, a few tough cowboys around Batchford don't count. You see it's rough, unsettled country, poor grazing desert you'd call it. No ranches or towns for miles. I've lived there since I was ten. And since I was fifteen, alone, except for my old ranch hand. We seldom went to Batchford, and never any farther. That is why I am sort of dazed. Everything's so different."

"No wonder. How much land have you?"

"I don't know how many acres, but miles. If it were irrigated it'd be valuable. We've run a hundred head of cattle until lately, then one thing and another cut my herd down. We grew mighty poor. Still we didn't starve. We raised corn, beans, potatoes. We had cows, pigs, chickens

—and more horses than cattle, I reckon. But there's no sale for horses in Idaho."

"You've come to the Wades' to make your home, Marigold said."

"Yes. Mr. Wade offered me a home. It was Marigold's doing. I love her for it. But I don't know how I'll make out. I want to work, but they don't want me to."

"I see. What'd you do with the ranch, the stock and your old ranch hand?"

"Left them. I couldn't sell out even if there were a buyer."

"Why not?"

"Be-because I reckon I'll want to go back someday—if I can't make a success of myself here."

"I hope you do. Now I'm going to tell you about my dad."

When Stanley finished his rather eloquent talk about his father, he saw tears in Lark's eyes. That was the climax of this morning's adventure. He made not the slightest effort to stem or gauge the warm, sweet wave of emotion that flowed over him.

"Dad wants to meet you. I told him what little I'd got from Marigold. He knew your father. He remembers your mother. Lark, have you Indian blood?"

"A little, on my grandmother's side . . . I would love to meet your father."

"Good. We'll arrange it soon. You see Dad has been in poor health for a long time. Some days, though, he's fine."

"Life is very sad. I remember my dad breaking slowly, right before my eyes. And oh, when he was gone—the difference!"

They were silent for some moments. Lark had struck a chord of memory for herself and one of apprehension for Stanley. The wind stirred the pines pleasantly, and brown needles sifted down. The horses were quiet. The sage rippled like a gray lake. Loneliness and solitude enfolded this isolated hill. It was a dreamy, restful place.

"I must go. It's been a long time, hasn't it?" spoke up Lark.

"Very short, I think. Do you want me to ride back with you, or part way?"

"Oh no, thank you. I'll make the run in no time."

"All right, Lark. I'll watch you ride away. I have my glasses, you know, so you must do your prettiest."

She rose and pulled on her sombrero and then her gloves. She was not little, as he had fancied. She came quite above his shoulder.

"Good-by—Stanley," she said, the shyness returning. "I'm glad I ran across you out here in the sage."

"Yes, it has been nice. I ride out here most every day. . . . Lark, do you think you might come tomorrow or the next day?"

"I—I reckon I might," she said hurriedly, and left him.

Stanley watched her vault into her saddle and gallop down the trail, where she put the mustang to a run and in a few minutes was only a fast-disappearing dot on the sage. When she was gone he lay back on the pine needles and gazed up through the green and into the blue.

A feeling, a suspension of thought, something which he had used to woo on the lonely hillside and which had for years been a stranger to him, subtly and unconsciously returned, only making itself known afterward. It had to do with his boyhood, far back, and was not a recollection of events, but a vague, sweet, dreamy condition of the senses.

At length he sat up. The field glasses lay at his feet. Had he lain there only a moment or for a long time? There was no way to tell, but he believed it had been long. And if Lark Burrell had not directly induced this spell, the simplicity of her, the almost childlike intangible something he could not name, most assuredly had done so. He felt an absurd gratitude. By that he acknowledged and measured a certain unhappy mental burden which he had borne for months. To be rid of that for a little while, even though he was not conscious of it until afterward, to have come through that to the old youthful enchantment, was something to be grateful for.

But what had his senses grasped during this interval? Only the sailing white clouds across the blue sky, the

quivering and soughing of the pine-needle foliage, the
protection of the black-trunked, black-branched trees,
the warmth of the sun on his face and the thick mat under
his shoulders, the mingled spicy odor of pine and sage—
these, and physical things that he could go on naming indefinitely, had been all that had occupied his mind. But to
feel them again, as of old, their sweetness and beauty,
their relation to the remote past, this was what charmed
him so. Right there a connection between Lark Burrell
and the cherished dreams of his boyhood had been estab-
lished. Marigold Wade had never roused any associations
that included his mother, or his barefoot days, his watching his image in still, deep pools, his hours on the windy
sage hillsides.

"I see my finish. If I meet that girl again—" he
thought, and broke off because there was no *if*. He would
meet her. If she did not ride out again to the sage he
would hunt for her. Marigold had so many times taunted
him: "Why don't you play around as I do? We'll be married a long time and dead longer." He had often wondered what she would do if he accepted her challenge.
But that had held no appeal for him.

Once off the slope he let Boots cut loose at his own
pace. Wherefore a half-dozen miles flashed by in a blur
of sage. He was home in time for lunch.

"Stan, what's thet cowboy Blanding out here for?"
were the first words with which his father greeted him.

"I don't know. Is he here?"

"Shore. Rode out early this mornin' an' hasn't left yet."

"Was he alone?"

"He had two or three fellows with him."

"Maybe he wants to make a drive for wild horses over
Sage Hill."

"Wal, I shouldn't wonder. An' if he does you block it."

"Sure I will, Dad. But what have you against Hurd
Blanding? He appears to stand well with the Wades."

"Humph. I've got enough," growled the old man.

Stanley made his thoughtful way back to the bunkhouse, which was a long, one-story, many-roomed building opposite the barns. Horses stood, heads down, at the

hitching rail; and there was a buckboard where it could not be easily seen. It turned out to be one of the Wades', Marigold's in fact, the one in which she had driven Lark and him back from town. Either Blanding had appropriated it for a while, as cowboys had a habit of doing, or Marigold had lent it to him. Whichever way it was, Stanley did not like it. He was tired of a lot of things.

He went into the messroom, where a dozen or more cowboys were eating at a long table. Several of these men, besides Blanding, did not belong to the Weston ranch. Having been trained by his father, Stanley had never gotten too friendly with his help. He was easygoing and kind, but he insisted on discipline, and he did not have any use for a drinking cowboy. His own foreman, Howard, had transgressed of late, after repeated warnings; and Stanley thought this might be a favorable time to talk forcibly to him, especially if he were bent on any deals with Blanding.

"Howdy, men," replied Stanley, in reply to their greeting. "What's up?"

There followed a scraping of boots. Howard coughed in a rather embarrassed fashion, and answered: "Blanding's wantin' some help on a wild-horse drive."

Stanley lifted a heavy boot to the edge of the bench and leaned his elbow on his knee, while he took a cool stare at the handsome Blanding. At first sight of this cowboy Stanley had been conscious of a boiling in his blood.

"Hello, Blanding. Did you ride over?"

"Naw, we drove over," returned the cowboy easily.

"Did you steal the buckboard?" went on Stanley, welcoming an opportunity like this.

Blanding's laconic assurance suffered a blight. The question struck like a blow. A dark red surged across his clean, tanned face and, receding, left it white.

"No, Mr. Weston, I didn't steal the buckboard!" he retorted. "Marigold lent it to me."

"Marigold! What business has a hired hand to call Miss Wade by her first name?"

The lightning leaped in Blanding's cold, hard gray eyes. In the passion of them he betrayed more than temper at the arraignment proffered. He had reason for resentment, aside from the wounding of his vanity.

"What business is it of yours?" returned Blanding insolently. He showed not the least physical fear; also, there was something in his mind that gave him a mastery here.

"Blanding, I'm not quite sure yet, or I would tell you," declared Stanley. "But I'll say this. You get off my ranch. Is that clear to you?"

The cowboy leaped to his feet, sending the bench crashing backward and upsetting two of the men. His hair stood up like a mane. His eyes were steel fire.

"Hell, yes, that's clear. But it's not clear why you insult me before your own outfit," returned Blanding hotly.

"Take it any way you want."

"All right, Weston. I take it you're sore at me because Marigold Wade—"

"Shut your mouth!" interrupted Stanley, thumping his boot to the floor and taking long strides to carry him within reaching distance of the cowboy. Stanley well knew that he was going to hit him, and further restraint seemed impossible. Controlling physical violence had long been trained into him, but the flood of his anger was new and unexpected.

"Well, I guess not, Weston," flared Blanding, in whom passion now had the upper hand. "You can't make a monkey out of me. Not even in your own back yard!"

"Go ahead, then," Stanley flung back at him contemptuously. "Give yourself away—that you haven't the first instincts of a gentleman."

"Weston," rasped Blanding, his lips curving in scorn, "you've no call on earth to insult me."

"We don't agree, Blanding."

Then the cowboy, true to his egotism and his hate, pushed a livid face closer to Stanley.

"But you bet your sweet life you've call to be jealous!"

How true that taunt was Stanley realized from more than the hot triumph in Blanding's voice. It was worse than he had feared. He wavered an instant. Then loyalty and manhood, and the jealousy Blanding had seen all too readily, united in one tremendous impulse. Stanley swung on the cowboy, and knocked him thudding to the floor. Blanding lay motionless. Then suddenly the messroom was in an uproar.

"Take him out," thundered Stanley. Blanding's comrades, with the help of others, made short work of that job. Then, when the men shuffled in again, closing the door, Stanley accosted Howard.

"What about this wild-horse drive?"

"Nothin' to fuss over, boss," returned the foreman nervously. "Blanding wanted me an' some of our outfit in the job. Seems he's had a row with young Wade."

"Did you agree to go with Blanding on that drive?"

"Yes, sir."

"Without asking my permission?"

"Why, I reckoned you'd be all for it. Riddin' the range of a lot of riffraff."

"Howard, the riffraff isn't all out on the sage. You were supposed to be working for me. Now pack your stuff and beat it."

"You're firin' me?" ejaculated the foreman, incredulous and dismayed.

"Yes. And anyone else who agreed to go in with Blanding."

"None of the boys agreed. He'd asked several, an' they was arguin' about their share."

"Very well, then. We'll let it go at that. I'll send your check down."

Stanley strode out to the house, thinking grimly of what choice material he had supplied for the gossips of Wadestown. A fight always exhilarated him—reminiscent of his old football days. He had not a regret for his violence. That conceited lady-killer had played right into his hands. Blanding was only a coarse cowboy, without wit, tact or any semblance of fine feeling. What a fool Marigold had been! Stanley, bitter as he was, inevitable as he felt the coming issue, remained loyal. Marigold had only played with the cowboy, flirted with him—led him on to amuse herself.

"Oh, but won't she be furious!" he ejaculated gleefully.

Later, in the living room, his observant father remarked: "Son you went out a while ago draggin' yourself, with a clouded face. Now you show up whistlin' an' otherwise bright. What come off?"

"Dad, I broke loose," laughed Stanley.

"Humph. It was about time. Did you block the wild-horse drive?"

"I sure did, as far as our range and Sage Hill are concerned."

"An' what else?"

"Well, I fired Howard."

"Say, son, you surprise me. You're wakin' up. Thet loafer ought to have been fired long ago. Anythin' else?"

"Yes, Dad. I took a crack at Hurd Blanding."

"You don't say!" The old man's manifest pleasure worked powerfully upon Stanley, inciting him to tell the particulars of the meeting. The recital, however, operated to inflame his father more against Marigold.

"She's ruined you, son. It's her fault," he raved.

"Hardly that, Dad."

"But it'll be town talk, this very night."

"I daresay. But a little fact is no worse than the usual gossip."

"Did you believe Blanding?" asked the old rancher stormily. "He shore must have been drunk or crazy to brag thet way aboot a woman, before a crowd of men, unless—"

"Dad, Blanding wasn't lying," replied Stanley. "I probably had call to be jealous of him. I knew it. And I was, though it seems to have died a violent death. But just how much reason I have, I can't see. Not much, I reckon. He is a conceited jackass. He thinks he's what cowboys call a lady-killer. I suspect that women have spoiled him. He's a wonderful-looking fellow. But I know that Marigold has only flirted with him, as she has with other fellows."

"How do you know thet?" asked old Weston bluntly.

"Why, Dad, I couldn't conceive of anything else," retorted Stanley, suddenly hot under the collar.

"Ahuh. Wal, you're young an' like your mother. She

couldn't believe bad of nobody. I reckon it's a good trait in human nature. But son, if I ever had thet, it shore got stung out of me."

6

THE AFTERMATH of Stanley's encounter with Blanding and Howard came the following morning, when Stanley went out to get his horse. He was informed by Morgan, an old ranch hand who had been with the Westons for years, that three of the cowboys had quit and left with Howard.

"Good riddance, Hank," replied Stanley. "We had too many in the outfit anyhow."

"Wal, mebbe so. We shore had too many drifters in our outfit."

"I'm not surprised at that, but I am at Howard being strong enough to take those boys with him, especially Price."

"Stan, it's not Howard's influence, but Hurd Blanding's. Thet fellow's got somethin' up his sleeve, an' it's not cowpunchin'!"

"Blanding? Oh, he's up in the air because he made some money out of that wild-horse drive."

"Mebbe it's thet, only I'm not so sure. The best thing you did around this range was to slug Blanding an' fire Howard."

Stanley rode away with considerably less pleasurable stir and expectation than he had felt before encountering Morgan. He did not like that suggestion of untoward events shaping themselves without his knowledge. But this evidently was a fact. He had not been the kind of boss who pried into the lives of his cowboys. He had shirked any deliberate interference with the foreman's running of the outfit. There were around eleven thousand head of stock wearing the Weston brand, not a great number for such an immense range, nevertheless, a big herd of cattle. Stanley's father had advised holding on until fall, despite Wade and other ranchers selling out on the unprecedented rise in price to ten cents a pound on the hoof. Old Weston seldom made mistakes, and he predicted the price would go higher.

Halfway out to the lone hill, Stanley, remembering the purpose and hope of this ride, dismissed his problems from his mind, and thought of Lark Burrell. Would she come? And he had to laugh at his keen desire to meet this cousin of Marigold's again.

He arrived at the hill in good time and, leaving his horse—a white one this time—standing out in the open, he repaired to the spot that would henceforth be a favorite with him. He tried to forget Marigold and win back the pleasurable mood of yesterday. However, he was not successful. Lark didn't come.

Stanley waited several hours, considerably longer than was needful. His disappointment was as keen as had been his anticipation. He wondered what had kept Lark. He would try again the following morning. On the way back to the ranch house he considered riding into town, but he decided against that. He was not in particularly good spirits.

Before reaching home, however, he encountered one of the Weston farm wagons and several cowboys, one of whom, Landy Elm, was mounted.

"Howdy, Landy, I'll ride along with you." He liked this cowboy, who was the son of a farmer, and had gone to school with Stanley. Landy was a blond young giant, a fine horseman, an industrious, sober fellow who had recently married a Wadestown girl.

"I'm just fine, Stan," replied Elm, and fell in along with Stanley in front of the wagon.

"I didn't see you in the bunkhouse yesterday," remarked Stanley.

"No. I was in town after grain."

"Hear anything?"

"Sure did, Stan. It was all over town last night."

"What was?"

"The row you had. Howard, Ross and Bell were sure painting Wadestown red last night. Sam Price was with them at first, but he wasn't drunk. And I heard he quit them and went home."

"Did you see Blanding?"

"Yes. He was at the station. Had a tooth busted loose or something, and was real unhappy. Report was out Blanding had been kicked by a horse."

Stanley laughed. "I'm the horse, Landy."

"Doggone! I wondered."

Whereupon Stanley briefly related what had happened in the bunkhouse.

"Well! That's far different from what's going the rounds in town," declared Elm. "The talk had to do with a big row about Blanding's wild-horse drive, but nothing was said about you punching him. Howard swore he quit and took three of our outfit with him. They tried to bully me into quitting. And they swear they'll comb our range for wild horses."

"I don't suppose there's any law to prevent them."

"Not written law, but I'll tell you, Stan, I'll be darned if I'd stand for it."

"Landy, do you think you could run our outfit?"

"I'll say I could," replied the cowboy eagerly.

"Very well, you take a whack at Howard's job."

"Doggone! Stan, do you mean for me to be foreman?"

"Yes. Come up to the house tonight and we'll talk it over with Dad. I think he'll approve. By the way, did you see any of the Wades?"

"Sure. Saw El last night at the station. Said howdy to him. Stan, I don't believe he's got much use for the Weston outfit. He's pretty thick with Blanding, or was. There's a rumor they've split over the wild-horse deal. . . . And I saw Marigold, too, yesterday afternoon in the saloon."

"Of course she wasn't alone there?"

"No, sure she wasn't. She—I—there was a crowd, you know, and I didn't take particular notice," returned Elm hastily.

Stanley did not press the question, for if Elm had declared outright that Blanding was in that crowd he could not have told him more clearly.

It seemed to Stanley that the following hours were long and fraught with something expectant and dismaying. Even his slumber was disturbed by a dream in which Lark Burrell saved him from a catastrophe, the nature of which did not clarify itself.

He reached the rendezvous next day long before it was time for Lark to appear. How eagerly he scanned the gray sage! No rider, no moving speck on the horizon! Whereupon he had recourse to the field glasses. Instantly he picked up a light-colored horse six or eight miles away. A strange tumult of sudden relief, delight and fear assailed him!

"Stan, you're a little off form," he thought. But it was no use to accuse himself of contrary mood. He might have had that on the way out here. But not now! He was aroused as Marigold had not aroused him for years. How strongly he wanted to see this Idaho girl again! It bothered him, and then, when he actually thought about it, he resented his dismay and was honest with himself. This day might not only tell a great deal about what had happened to him, but be potent for the future.

Stanley looked through the glasses, watching the cream-colored mustang grow larger and his rider assume shape. He surely could run. Presently Stanley laid aside the glasses. At two miles he could discern horse and rider plainly. A few more minutes passed, somehow strangely tedious to Stanley, despite the rapid approach of the mustang. At half a mile's distance he caught a bit of red color, fluttering at the neck, waving in the wind like Lark's hair. She was wearing a red scarf. There was other color, too, about her, and not dark, as on the previous occasion. Chaps was on a dead run, stretched out, level and beautiful.

Lark's horse lifted his head, breaking his wonderful gait because he was being pulled. He broke to a gallop, then a lope, then a trot, which he was slowing as Lark turned him up the slope, at a point even with the white horse. It was still a good two hundred yards down the gradual incline to the trail. Lark walked the mustang. She allowed him to nip at the grass, as Stanley's horse was doing. But every step brought Lark closer and closer. Stanley leaned there against the pine, waiting. She saw him. She waved her hand. But he did not wave back. He felt transfixed there, though he yearned to rush down the hill to meet her. At last she reached the white horse, and there she dismounted, about fifty steps below the edge of the timber. She loosened the cinch, she patted the mustang, she lingered until evidently there was nothing further to linger over. Then she turned up the slope. Her head was bare and she did not carry the old sombrero. A new gray sweater, that was buttoned up to the flowing red scarf, set off her shapeliness to surprising advantage.

"Hello, Stanley," she called gaily. "Have you turned into another pine tree?"

"Hello, Lark!" he called in reply, and his sonorous voice, or its deeper, richer note, suddenly made her face match the scarf in hue. Such a blush Stanley could not recall ever having seen. It was a great wave of scarlet.

Perhaps it helped Stanley on his way, as a tumultuous moment later her eyes did, but not until she got clear up to him did he realize the truth. Then his reaction was swift. It was as if he had been released from binding emotions, to find his old easy self. She hesitated, confused, out of breath, yet unmistakably glad, and held out an ungloved hand.

Stanley took it, and held it while he gazed down upon her, singularly alive to her charm.

"I waited here all morning yesterday. You did not come," he said with reproach.

"Oh, I—I couldn't. I'm sorry, Stanley. I—"

"Why couldn't you?"

"I—it was on account—of Marigold," Lark began haltingly, and ended that way.

"Did you tell her you met me the other day?"

"Stanley, I meant to, but I—I didn't," she said shamefacedly. "I went to her room on purpose—to tell her. But she was cross—different, somehow—and I just didn't, and this morning she wasn't up." She hesitated a moment, and then, as if to be honest with herself: "But I don't believe I'd have told her, anyway. . . . Should I have, Stanley?"

"Not if it embarrassed you. Don't bother your head about it, Lark. I'll tell her."

"Oh, well, that's all right then," she replied, brightening. "Stanley, is it necessary—to hold my hand all this while?"

"Very necessary," he said coolly. "Come, let's sit down."

"You're different, too, this morning," returned the girl, drawing her hand away and looking at him dubiously.

"Am I cross?"

"Not that. But you don't speak and look like you did the other day."

"That may well be true, Lark. Perhaps I am more my real self today."

"I don't know yet but what I like you best the other way. Aren't you going to ride with me?"

"Of course I am, presently. Just now though I want to sit here and talk."

She did not come very willingly, but her reluctance, and the fact that despite it she could not resist him, were inexpressibly sweet to Stanley. They sat down on the fragrant pine needles, where the sun through the foliage above cast gold and shade all about them.

"There are your glasses," she said, seeing them. "You forgot them?"

"Yes, I forgot them the other day."

"You used them this morning?"

"Yes. I found you right off out there in the sage. So I guess I'll want them to see you coming again."

"Am I—coming again?"

"Aren't you?"

"Stanley, are you asking me to—to meet you out here again—alone?"

"Asking you? I should smile I am. Lark, you made me feel like a boy the other day. I was happier than I've been for years."

"How—strangely you talk! . . . Oh, I'm glad if I did. But, Stanley, I—I don't understand you."

"Lark, I don't understand myself. But that's a lie. I do. . . . Lark, tell me all that's happened to you."

"Oh, goodness! I couldn't," she replied laughing. "I'd like to—so much I dare not."

"Well, I see I'll have to question you."

"Must I answer?"

"Absolutely," he said, and leaned on his elbow so that he could obtain a better view of her face. She sat looking out at the sage, presenting only her profile to him. "Do you like Marigold?"

"I think I love her."

"Do you think you will keep on loving her?"

"If I love anyone, it's forever," she retorted.

"Excuse me, Lark. Anyone is marvelously lucky. . . . Have you seen through Marigold yet?"

"What do you mean?" she asked, as much surprised as shocked.

A perverse spirit, for which he could not account, urged Stanley on.

"Well, I agree with you that Marigold is beautiful, generous, sweet, bewildering, happy, gay and all that sort of thing. But have you found out yet that she's vain and willful?"

"I have not," rejoined Lark stoutly.

"Have you found out she's a flirt?" went on Stanley, as cool as ever, though this query found heat deep within him. Still, interrogation of this girl was tantalizingly full of charm.

"Stanley! Aren't you ashamed?"

"Well, yes . . . but have you found it out?"

"I wouldn't tell if I had," answered Lark, with hot cheeks.

"All right, then. Have you found out she's extravagant?"

"Yes, indeed. But not selfishly. She bought the same kind of clothes that she wears, for me, and, Stanley, right here let's understand each other," she declared, as if driven. "You're not the same today. You're more like the rest of the young men. .... Oh, please don't look insulted. I—I know you're not. I only said more like—a little. .... But don't tease me."

"I'm far from teasing you, Miss Burrell. I am sure going to take you out someday."

"With Marigold?"

"No. Alone."

"Where?"

"Well, first to a dance, Saturday night. It's pretty nice up till eleven o'clock. Then I'll take you home."

Lark's expression betrayed both rapture and fright.

"Marigold took me with her last night," returned Lark, presently. "Oh, it was exciting. I'd like it, if I could have gotten over something."

"Did you dance?" asked Stanley darkly.

"I tried. Marigold gave me lessons at home. I felt so light I could have flown. It was easy to keep time to the music. But it wasn't easy to—to be hugged."

"I was coming to that. Who hugged you?"

"Ellery Wade first, and most barefacedly. He laughed when I objected. So I—I just quit dancing with him. I told Marigold. She swore at him."

"Lark, we're getting somewhere. Let's dispose of El Wade. Of course he has made a play for you at home?"

"You mean waylaid me—tried to—?"

"Just that."

"Yes, he has. And it's bad for me because his mother thinks he's perfect. I detest him."

"Whom else did you dance with?"

"Charlie Fairchild. I liked him."

"Charlie's a nice chap. Whom else, Lark?"

"Mr. Barnes. He was jolly. I didn't do so well with him."

"Barnes is all right. Anyone else?"

"Coil Bruce. I'd met him at the ranch, the very morning I rode out here first. He's one of the cowboys. I liked him best."

"Oh, you did? How much is best?"

"Are you my big brother—that you question me so?"

"I sure am not. Well, Bruce is a regular fellow, I'm bound to admit. Clean, fine boy. Whom else, lady?"

"Young man named Trumbell. Tall, good looking. Oh, he could dance!"

"Not Vic Trumbell?" asked Stanley, frowning.

"Yes, they called him Vic."

"Ahuh. And how about Vic?"

"Well, he held me too tight, until I said, 'Say, Mr. Trumbell, if you want me to dance you'll have to let me breathe.' He laughed, too, but after that he behaved. I never met such a wonderful talker!"

"Lark, listen. Vic won't do. Not for you. I'll sure call Marigold for throwing you in his way."

"But why, Stanley? He—he asked to come to see me, and I said I'd see."

"Nothing doing. Someone must take care of you, and if Marigold won't do it, I will. Do you hear that, my little lark from Idaho?"

"I hear you, yes," she replied demurely, and gave him a side flash of dark eyes.

"Do you wish me to tell you why Vic Trumbell won't do?" Stanley asked, a little coldly.

"No. But, Stanley, what'll I do when Marigold introduces me to—to—?"

"You can't help yourself. But you can be on your guard. . . . Lark, did they have anything to drink?"

"Yes."

Stanley hesitated. He hated to make further queries for Lark's sake and strangely for his own.

"Lark, did you drink?" he asked thickly.

"Stanley, need you ask that?"

"I had to. . . . Lark, promise me you will never drink."

"I don't need to promise that. I never did and I never will."

"All the same, promise me. I feel rather deeply about it. I'll explain someday. You're only a—a youngster. And all this is so new."

"Why of course I promise you," she said shyly.

He found her hand and squeezed it without glancing at her. Then, though he relaxed his grip, he did not drop it.

Lark's face wore the trancelike, vaguely troubled look of a girl drifting down an enchanted river, the peril of which was hidden, yet which seemed strong in the chafing, murmuring current.

"Now to make a clean breast of your vicissitudes. What else happened? I mean disturbing." Stanley seemed driven to find out everything that had happened to Lark.

"Stanley, the worst so far was three mornings ago—the day of my first ride," she began, with growing frankness. She wanted to confide in him. "I wore these jeans, and my old blouse and sombrero. You remember. Well, at the barn I ran into three cowboys throwing dice. One of them —Coil Bruce—saw me, took me for a boy. I said I wanted a horse. They didn't pay any attention to me. I enjoyed fooling them, until their talk made me want to get out. The oldest of the three—Hurd Blanding—took me for a smart-aleck kid and he threw a chunk of wood at me. Hit me on the foot and it hurt. Then I broke out. You should have seen the faces of those cowboys. . . . But Blanding was a slick one. He didn't let any grass grow under his feet. Tried to make me believe he knew I was a girl all the time. He shoved the other two away and began to walk me up and down the barn to see the horses. Even before I talked to this cowboy I hated him. Because he was the one who sold the wild horses for chicken feed. But I didn't let on. I wanted to see what he'd say and do. He hung on to my arm. Made me burn, but still I didn't let on. . . ."

The expression on Stanley's face made Lark falter. However, his "Go on!" was so urgent that she continued.

"When I saw Chaps I sort of forgot Mr. Blanding. I woke up quick. He pulled off my sombrero. He kept getting himself closer. He had big, handsome, hard eyes. Suddenly he bent over me. Stanley, the fool meant to kiss me! . . . I gave him a shove and told him to keep his hands off me. . . . That—that's about all. He was sure surprised, but persisted some some. I saddled Chaps myself and rode out here, where I met you."

"When did you see Blanding again?" asked Stanley, fortifying himself.

"I haven't seen him since. Do you know him, Stanley?"

"A little."

"He's not just a regular cowboy, is he? I hear he came to Washington from California. Is that true?"

"I reckon so, Lark," rejoined Stanley constrainedly. The girl was staring at him with penetrating eyes.

"Well, why don't you tell me I'm not to have anything to do with Hurd Blanding?" asked Lark almost casually.

It did not matter how unsophisticated she was—here spoke the subtle femininity of a woman. It baffled Stanley. He simply could not answer that, and sustained a faint, sickening fear that she knew why. This broke the spell of the hour. He let go of her hand, amazed that he had retained it so long, and more than amazed that she had permitted him the privilege.

"You needn't tell me, for I won't of my own accord," she added.

"Lark, may I tell you something?" he asked with emotion.

"Sure. I—I guess so. I'd rather you told me things than asked questions."

"You're a wonderful girl."

"Is that *your* line, too, Stanley?" she countered, half banteringly, half regretfully. "These boys all have lines, Marigold warned me."

"No, Lark, I haven't any line. I guess I haven't character either," he returned, feeling a sudden dejection.

"Oh, I've hurt your feelings," she flashed instantly. "I didn't mean that, Stanley. I knew you hadn't a line. I trust you. I want you to help me in this new life I've adopted. If you don't I—I shall fail."

"Thanks, Lark. That's better," he said, and the wave of dejection vanished. "Then you don't put me in a class with Blanding, Trumbell and Ellery Wade?"

She uttered a sharp little laugh of derision. "I think you're wonderful."

"You do? Then if you think I'm wonderful and if I think you're wonderful—it's all really very wonderful, isn't it?" The depth of feeling in Stanley's voice overcame the banality of his words.

"Yes," she whispered, her head dropping. "But please let's not talk any more about us. It—it upsets me. And I haven't told you anything yet."

"Maybe you haven't. But go ahead."

"Stanley, I hear a lot. I'm not much on talk, though my exhibition here may not indicate that. But I've ears. And the particular thing I want to tell you is about another wild-horse drive. Perhaps you've heard."

"Not much. Just mention of it."

"Well, as I've figured out, this Blanding, who's at the head of it, is a pretty clever fellow. He's got the Indians on his side. I heard Ellery Wade tell his father that Blanding had double-crossed him. They've split. Mr. Wade forbade any of his cowboys to take part in the drive. Blanding gave up his job with the Wade ranch. He intends to make a business of this catching wild horses to be slaughtered. Oh, but it makes me furious! . . . Well, Blanding is having trouble getting riders. So he has asked a number of the town boys to help. A lot of girls are going, too. They'll camp, ride and have a regular picnic. Marigold is crazy to go, I reckon. First I thought I couldn't, possibly, but I got an idea. . . ." She broke off abruptly, then asked, "Will you go, Stanley?"

"Go! Will I? Lark, your perspicuity is nil," said Stanley.

"What's that?" asked Lark blankly.

"I mean you don't understand. You've a beautiful little head, all shining with curly locks, but I fear it's empty."

"I wish you'd talk sense," declared Lark impatiently.

"Lark, I'll be overjoyed to go. I don't know of anything that would please me so."

"But, Stanley, *you* wouldn't help Blanding?" she cried, startled.

"Oh, then, you don't want me to go?" inquired Stanley in pretense.

"Yes. If you don't I—I shall play off sick. But if you do go and help Blanding I'll *be* sick. It'll just break my heart, Stanley. . . . Can't you see? You're the only help I have up here in this terrible country."

"Shake hands on that," returned Stanley, suddenly thrusting out his hand.

"On what?"

"I'm your *only* help!"

"Oh! . . ."

They clasped hands. Stanley did not know what she discovered in his eyes, but in hers, before they wavered and fell, he saw courage, faith, and shadowy, unconscious yearning.

"Now, let's ride," she whispered, breaking his clasp.

They rode up to the top of the wooded hill from which Stanley showed her Sage Hill Ranch, and then down on the other side. They raced through the sage. He accompanied her halfway home, and at last reined his horse to say good-by.

"Tomorrow morning?" he asked.

She met his glance appealingly, wonderingly, abruptly forced to think again.

"Stanley."

"Lark?"

"I want to, Stanley, but I don't feel that I'm playing fair with Marigold."

For a moment or two Stanley did not reply. Then he said slowly, "You're right, Lark. I'll call for you tomorrow evening."

She had no word for him. Her dark, shining eyes dilated with sudden misgiving. Then Stanley, his conscience smarting, his exultation soon smothering it, spurred his horse and rode homeward. Presently he turned, to find that she still sat motionless in her saddle, watching him. Waving, he rode on, and when again he looked he saw a black dot moving across the sage.

Stanley went early to the Wade home the next morning, and asked for Marigold. A subtle change in her, and an unexpected kiss of greeting made him waver, but did not deter him from his purpose.

"Marigold, I am taking Lark out tonight," he said at once.

"You are?—That's sweet of you, Stan," she replied,

with thoughtful gaze. "She's a dear kid. . . . Have you seen her lately?"

"I came across her the first day she rode out on the sage. She should not have been alone. Then I asked her to come again, and met her."

"Big-brother stuff, or are you—"

"Yes." Stanley interrupted, with a cool laugh. "Somebody must help Lark to find herself in this new life, and it may as well be I."

"You know I'd rather have you do it than Ellery, or any other boy I know. But, Stan—" Her eyes darkened ponderingly. "Lark is only a kid. She might fall terribly in love with you."

"I'll risk it!" he exclaimed bitterly. "Marigold, I've another thing to confess. Have you heard of my fight with Blanding?"

"Fight!" She paled decidedly and seemed startled. "No . . . So that is what happened. . . . Stan, what was it about?"

Stanley briefly narrated the story of his clash with the cowboy, putting the emphasis on the wild-horse drive.

"And he told you I lent him my wagon? He took it!" Marigold exclaimed angrily.

"I didn't believe him—or the implication that you flirted with him."

"You wouldn't, Stan. . . . All the same it's true," she returned, meeting his eyes bravely. But she flushed.

"What did you do, Marigold? I always knew you were a flirt, ever since our school days. But surely—"

"It began—that way," she said frankly. "Hurd is a handsome devil. I have played around with him some. . . . Kissed him. But no more, Stan."

"No more? It seems to me you went quite far," he returned coldly, amazed that he felt no hurt. "Marigold, how did you come to go so far?"

"I liked him. He fascinates me," she admitted.

Stanley paced the drawing room, gazed out of the window, and closed the door, finally confronting her again.

"You always were game," he went on, trying to be

calm. "Some girls would have deceived me. . . . If it has gone so far—would you like to break our engagement?"

"Stanley!" she cried, and suddenly she clasped him. "You would not break with me?"

"If you wanted it—yes."

"But I don't want it," she rejoined hurriedly. She seemed strange, driven, not the old Marigold at all. Still, it had been long since there had been any deep exchange of feelings between them.

"Marigold, I would not jilt you," he said gravely. "We have been engaged a long time. I can scarcely recall when it was not understood that we were to marry. All our friends, relatives, our families look upon it as something settled . . . Am I reasonable to ask you to marry me soon, or at least, if you will not, to cut out this sort of thing you are doing?"

"Stanley, you are the best—Oh, I *am* ashamed," she murmured incoherently, and threw her arms around his neck. "I—I *do* love you—more than anyone. But I don't want to be tied down yet—to live out there in the sage— to have kids. . . . Please don't force me."

"I would not force you, or even insist," he replied, more than ever surprised at the unexpected warmth and agitation in her. "Nevertheless—"

She closed his lips with a kiss. "Give me more time, darling."

"Time! . . . Marigold, *if* I forced you, would you marry me soon?"

"Yes."

"When?"

"Tomorrow! . . . But, Stan, if you want to—to get the best of me—to keep my love—don't rush me," she replied poignantly, and hid her face upon his breast.

Stanley held her, conscious of conflicting emotions. He could not understand her, and in the bewilderment of the moment could only reply that he never would rush her.

"Let's wait till fall anyway. I don't know *what* I want," she said, and released herself gently. "Only I can't bear restraint. Will you stand for it, this way, for a while?"

"Yes. But I don't think it wise."

"How can one love and be wise? . . . Stan, you are wonderful. I wish I were more . . . I'll run now before I bawl."

She kissed him and fled. Stanley went to the window and gazed out across the ranch, out to open country. That Marigold seemed to love him, somewhat as of old, touched him deeply, and softened him. But it only added to his trouble. He realized that something sweet and beautiful which had lately come into his life should now fade and leave him cold. But it did not. A rebellious warmth remained in his heart.

7

IT WAS early Saturday afternoon, and Lark hurried home from her errand. She had seen Hurd Blanding on the street and did not want to encounter him. Once out of the business area of Wadestown, she had a mile walk along a tree-lined road to the Wade ranch. The last part was uphill and a good climb, which none of the Wades ever made on foot. But Lark liked walking, if she could be alone.

The day was fine, sunny and warm, with a hint of May in the air. She had missed her horseback ride that morning, so much that it added considerably to a guilty conscience. But greatly as Lark loved to ride, it was not only that which had made the mornings glamorous and fateful. To miss seeing Stanley Weston had given her a pang that was illuminating and dismaying. She fought off the bad thought that she had fallen in love with him. She told herself it was only that she had been wildly excited and overcome by the events of the week since her arrival at Wade Ranch. To consider seeing Stanley again—this very day—and go out with him made her giddy and fearful.

There was relief in the thought that probably it would not come to pass.

Entering the yard, Lark saw a wagon that apparently had just arrived, for dust sifted in sunny patches between the trees. It was a bright new wagon, the identical one in which she had seen Blanding in the village.

Lark hurried under the trees to the side entrance of the big house. The living room was vacant. There did not appear to be anyone around. As Lark passed into the hall she heard a faint sound—a rustle, and then something like a gasp. In another second she saw into the library. Hurd Blanding stood just inside, his handsome, hawklike head bent over Marigold, her arm around his neck.

Lark slipped noiselessly up the stairs to her door, which she managed to open and close and lock quietly. She dropped her parcel and threw off her bonnet, feeling weak and paralyzed from the shock. The scene she had inadvertently witnessed explained what had been so baffling about her cousin. Lark felt stunned, horrified. She had really come to love Marigold. She understood many things now—the bantering of the cowboys, the hints, the connecting of Marigold's name with Blanding's, the elusive sort of intimacy which Lark had observed between them on two occasions.

Then suddenly she remembered Stanley—that he loved Marigold and was engaged to marry her. Lark writhed and burned at that.

Grief followed close upon her rage and scorn. She wept, and after the paroxysm had subsided she got up to pace the floor. She realized that she was in a terrible predicament. She loved Stanley. In the tumult of the last hour she had confessed the thing to herself, changed it from a dream to stark truth. She knew Stanley loved Marigold and wanted to marry her. Had not her cousin laughingly told her how Stanley had coaxed, insisted, stormed that she marry him in June? But Marigold had refused.

"I'm having too much fun," Marigold had concluded that confidence. Fun! Lark was haunted by the picture of Marigold flattened in Blanding's arms. What did it mean?

Lark saw how slight was her knowledge of love and life. And this new world was an enigma. She tried to pierce the mystery. "Blanding is bad," Lark whispered to herself. "I *felt* that. But Marigold—she's only a vain, crazy girl who's carrying things too far. . . . Oh, dear, I don't know what to do to help poor Stanley."

Lark had long hours of conflicting emotions, of self-interogation and grave consideration of Marigold and her friends, of Stanley's plight and her own. The outcome was her decision that she must overcome herself in order to aid her cousin and Stanley. It might have been hard for Lark to keep her own secret, if all had been well with Stanley. But he was in danger of heartbreak and disgrace. How in the world she was ever going to save Marigold she had no idea, but she knew she could do something for Stanley.

Lark, now that she had her back to the wall and was fighting for someone else, experienced a strong presence of the spirit with which she had tackled the many stubborn problems of her ranch life in Idaho. They had been problems for a man and required cool nerve and intelligence. She made sure of herself. She grasped the old Lark to her breast and held her there.

To decide upon any momentous question was for Lark to act. The hour was late, as she could tell by the ruddy, darkening west. Marigold would be dressing. Lark opened her door and went down the hall to her cousin's room. She knocked.

"Wait till tomorrow, Mom. I don't want any more arguments with you today," answered Marigold in a languid voice.

"It's Lark. Please may I come in?"

"Oh, it's you. Sure you can."

Lark entered to find Marigold half clothed on the bed, and her room in colorful disorder. "Thought it was Mom, Lark. She's been nagging me about Hurd Blanding who was here, and I didn't want any more of it." Whereupon Marigold looked up. "Say, Lark, but you're pale. Do you feel well?"

"Marigold, when I came in this afternoon I saw you and Mr. Blanding," said Lark quietly.

"So it *was* you. I heard somebody. Thank heavens—What'd you see, Lark?"

"You—crushed in his arms."

"Crushed is the word. So that's what makes you look like that!"

Marigold laughed in cool, gay mirth. She had the open, guileless face of an angel, her blue eyes without a shadow. She looked straight up at Lark without surprise or shame.

"It was a shock, Marigold," said Lark gravely.

"So I see. Well, it needn't have been. He had just come back from town. He'd had a couple of drinks too many. Bought a new wagon—got another big order for wild horses. So he was excited. Grabbed me and kissed me. It's happened before. *I* couldn't help it. I couldn't stop him."

"Marigold, you had an arm round *his* neck."

"Did I? You have sharp eyes, Lark," returned Marigold, with a laugh not so spontaneous. "He put it there."

Lark waited a moment, conscious of despair.

"Is that all, Marigold?"

"That's all he did."

"I mean is *that* all you have to say?"

"Why, sure. What more can I say? I'm sorry you were shocked. But really it's nothing, honey. Only don't tell Stanley. He wouldn't understand. He's not fond of Hurd anyway."

"I won't tell Stanley," promised Lark, as quietly as she had begun this interview. "But I'll tell *you* something, cousin. Mr. Blanding tried the same on me."

"He *what?*" flashed Marigold, with blue fire blazing in the eyes that an instant before had been so languid and innocent.

Lark proceeded then to divulge to Marigold the full details of her first encounter with Blanding. During the recital, she caught only a fleeting glimpse of Marigold's face before it was averted, but that was long enough to see a dark clouding wave of red.

"I—I'm glad you didn't fall for him, Lark," Marigold replied, after what seemed a long pause. Her voice was neither strong nor steady. "They're all alike—these fellows. No wonder a girl . . . Much obliged for telling me. I'll give Mr Blanding a bad moment, believe me."

"I told Stanley, too."

"You did! Heavens! What did he have to say, Lark? He's a chivalrous one, always on the side of the poor, unprotected girl. It's a wonder he didn't hunt Hurd up again and really beat him up."

Then Marigold did a strange thing. She flung one slipper after the other, bang against the headboard of the bed. She swore. "—— ——liar! He told me—I'm glad Stanley beat him up—"

"What do you mean, Marigold? Did Stanley—?" asked Lark, too astonished to finish her query.

"Yes, and it served him right," retorted Marigold vehemently. Then she related the whole story to Lark. Apparently the telling assuaged her feelings, for she ended the tale with one of her usual flippant remarks.

Then she patted Lark kindly on the shoulder. "You're good, Lark," she said. "I'm glad Stan is taking you out tonight. I can trust *him* anyway. And you, too."

"Thank you, Marigold," replied Lark, in sudden relief.

"All right, honey. Beat it now, or I'll never get dressed."

Lark ran, relieved that Marigold took it so lightly. Marigold was too deeply engrossed in her own thoughts to be interested in Lark's affairs.

Dusk had fallen. The cool night air blew in. Lark sat at the open window a moment, letting the breeze fan her heated face. The sage plain appeared lonely and calling. Lark thought of home, and how welcome the solitude would have been just then! She closed the window, pulled down the blind, and lighting the lamp she faced this strange, scarlet-cheeked, fire-eyed image in consternation. Where was Lark Burrell? She must be dreaming.

Lark had just finished dressing when Marigold called gaily, "There's a man down here who says he is taking you to the dance tonight. Hurry up!"

Ellery burst into the hall. "Come on, Sis, let's go!"

"All right, see you at the dance, Stan."

She went out with her brother. The door slammed. Lark heard Ellery's light laughter as she came down the stairs.

Mr. Wade called from the living room, "Come in, Lark, and let us look you over."

Lark complied and was pleased at Mr. Wade's admiring greeting. Mrs. Wade's scrutiny was not so friendly.

"You look well," she said rather grudgingly. "I hope you appreciate Stanley's kindness in giving you this evening's pleasure."

"Oh, I do indeed," responded Lark, sure that no one but herself could guess how much.

Stanley stood in the living-room door, and as Lark turned to him she was just in time to see a rather odd expression pass from his face. Then he was leading her through the hall, and out on the porch.

He helped her into the buckboard and walked around to gather up the reins. In another moment they were off.

Soon they reached the town and tied up with numerous other wagons in front of the schoolhouse, where the dances were held. There were sounds of music and gaiety wafting out in the cool night air.

As they entered Lark noticed a long table on one side, laden with food, and chairs around the other walls.

"Here we are," said Stan. "Shall we dance for a while, or would you prefer to eat first?"

"Oh, let's dance now, and eat later," she exclaimed. She was acutely conscious of the battery of eyes leveled upon her. Far indeed was she from the indifference she feigned. The situation filled her with an inexplicable exultation, which, when she realized it, suffered instant eclipse. What if they could see that she was madly in love with Stanley Weston, fiancé of the generous cousin who had befriended her! But Lark, despite her qualms, kept up through pride and something else.

"See any fellow you'd rather have than me?" said Stan casually.

"Not one—yet. But I haven't seen them all," she rejoined, imitating him. Lark was discovering a hitherto unknown source of feminine protectiveness.

"Well, if you do, keep it a secret or there'll be murder. Hello—here comes Marigold."

Lark saw Marigold approaching. It seemed to Lark there were none to compare with her cousin. Marigold's fair beauty shone lustrously in the light. She was smiling. Her eyes were dark with excitement.

"Hello, Lark and Stan," she said gaily. "Will you join us? We have a table in the corner. I saved two places."

"Thanks, Marigold," replied Stanley. "I think we'll have a dance first. How about that, Lark?"

"Oh, indeed, I'd rather dance, unless Marigold insists," replied Lark hastily.

"All right . . . but Stan, how about dances? Those fellows are wild over Lark."

"Who, for instance?"

"Oh, Vic, and in fact all of them."

"Is Vic with you?"

"Yes."

"Marigold, I asked you not to go out with Vic Trumbell," said Stanley coolly.

"I know you did. But you're not my husband yet."

"I've observed that. . . . Thank you, but I decline to exchange dances with your partner. I won't absolutely monopolize Lark, so don't be concerned about her pleasure."

"Will I see you at home later?" asked Marigold. She was suave, almost flippant, but that did not deceive Lark. Her cousin had received a sudden, startling intimation, and it had come while she was looking at her fiancé.

"That depends upon when you come home. I shall not keep Lark out very late, certainly not after midnight."

"Well, then, on Monday. Of course you're going on the wild-horse picnic with us?"

"Yes, thanks, I'll be glad to go. What are the particulars—when, how, and where?"

"Dad is letting us have the chuck wagon. You'll need your camp outfit and horse. We'll be leaving the ranch sometime Monday, early enough to ride out to Brazon's Spring to camp."

"All right. But I may see you before!"

"Yes. Well, so long . . . Lark, have a good time, but don't believe all you see."

"I won't, cousin."

Marigold glided away in her blue gown, a compelling figure of grace and distinction. Stanley turned to Lark.

"Stanley," said Lark in a low voice, "Marigold is hurt."

"Hurt! What about?"

"About your bringing me here."

"Lord, no. Marigold's not jealous—and why should she be hurt, considering she is with Vic Trumbell?"

"She has no right to be, but that's not it. . . . Aren't you hurt, too, Stanley?"

He could not lie to those earnest eyes.

"Yes, I am. She has deliberately disregarded my wishes. Why, Lark, this Trumbell has the worst reputation in Wadestown."

"Oh, Stanley, why does Marigold go out with him?"

"I suppose it's because he's bright, gay—a raw-talking person. Wonderful dancer, as you know. Girls—so many of them—*like* fellows such as Trumbell and Blanding. I'm only half alive, so Marigold says."

"It's good I can think for myself, Stanley. You're surely very much alive to me," returned Lark.

"Thanks, Lark. That makes up for a lot. Well, let's dance and be happy."

He spoke merrily, though there was a tinge of bitterness in his voice. Lark resented Marigold's treatment of Stanley. She checked a hasty reply and put her attention to her dancing, until presently they decided to eat.

Lark had not yet experienced unalloyed pleasure in any meal to which she had sat down since her arrival in Wadestown. She had known how sadly deficient she was in the etiquette of these people and, in spite of Marigold's coaching, she was still uncomfortable at the table. With Stanley, however, she forgot her self-consciousness and was happy to be seated while he procured their plates.

"Stanley, I am hungry after all," she said brightly.

"Sure you are. It wouldn't be flattering to me if you lost your appetite."

"That's all you know."

Then the music drowned any further talk. A queer thing about this music, to Lark, was the fact that she could not keep her feet still. Most of the company at the tables dived pell-mell for the center of the room. Lark watched them, fascinated. The rhythmic movement, the flashing faces, the music, now loud and blatant, and then low and long-drawnout, the flickering candles, and the soft sliding shuffle of many feet—all these represented something to Lark that her past experience could not interpret for her. They were all young people. They lived in Wadestown or its vicinity. They had parents, sisters, brothers. They went to school and worked and idled.

For a while Stanley, noticing Lark's gravity and thoughtfulness, left her free to watch and think until the music began again. Then he danced with her, was witty and funny by turns, and then silent. During this interval did he once hold her ever so slightly closer? Lark could not be sure of anything. During the dance she drifted away. The end of it seemed a rude disruption.

"Lark, I'm not going to hog all the dances," announced Stanley. "There's several nice chaps who're gazing yearningly at you. Suppose I get some dances for you with them."

"If you like—but I'd far rather have you."

"All the same I'm going to play the game. I may dance once with Marigold, if she'll chuck her partner. Come on, let's go."

The ensuing hour passed swiftly and pleasantly for Lark. She had three new partners, young men who were nice and merry, who did not confuse her, who thought of her entertainment. During these dances she never quite lost track of Stanley, though he danced but once, and that, the latter part of a number, with Marigold.

At its close they came up to Lark and her partner.

"Lark, you look positively radiant," declared Marigold. "How do you make yourself feel that way?"

"Oh, I've enjoyed myself."

"I'm glad, Lark," said Marigold kindly. "I'd have asked Stan long ago to bring you here, if I'd thought he'd do it. But he doesn't care much for this sort of thing. *I* can't get him to come here any more."

"Huh, you've tried very hard, Mari Wade, I don't think," retorted Stanley good-humoredly.

"Do you still mean to go home after this next, Stan?" asked Marigold.

"Yes."

"But it's so early. Don't take Lark home now. She's just beginning to come out of her shell."

"It's up to Lark," acceded Stanley.

"I'll be quite ready to go home—after one more."

That last dance seemed a farewell to Lark. She could not rid her mind of a melancholy premonition that this peculiar way of being happy was not for her. And toward the end of the dance she grew heavy in Stanley's arms.

"Let's stop, Stanley. Take me out—in the air," she begged. Stanley lost no time in getting their coats and hurrying out.

"What is it?" he asked solicitously.

"I don't know. Guess I just gave out—all of a sudden. I feel better now," she replied.

"It was close in there. But pull your coat up round your neck. You might get chilled. I'll drive slowly."

Lark had little to say on the way out to the ranch, and for that matter Stanley made no effort to maintain a conversation. He did not drive quite up to the house. Stopping in the moon-blanched shade of the big trees he turned to Lark, his face earnest, his lighter mood all gone.

"It's been wonderful, Lark. Dancing with you was just —well, never mind. But my conscience hurts me."

"On—account of—Marigold?" stammered Lark.

"Not at all," he answered quickly. "Marigold's behavior permits me free scope. I wasn't thinking of her, but of you."

"Stanley, why should your conscience hurt you—about me?"

"You seem to like that stuff, Lark. The excitement, the dancing, the music."

"Yes, I did. But only tonight, Stanley. Not the other

time. I'm only human. Tonight with you, I let myself go. It was heavenly."

"Lark, you were the prettiest, sweetest, most altogether charming girl I ever took anywhere in my life."

"Oh Stanley!"

She bade him a tremulous good night, went into the house and up to her room. The realization that she loved Stanley—and he loved Marigold—made her sob herself to sleep.

8

HORSE HEAVEN HILL was a mountain with two rounded peaks, the vast southern gray-green slopes of which converged in an amphitheater rolling away into the level sage. The whole south front of the mountain appeared to be a bowl of horse-shoe shape, tilted toward the open. The two points, leagues apart, descended in low timbered ridges to vanish on the floor of the valley.

All of the country, in its grays and greens and purples, indicated the influence of altitude, of a snow mantle in winter, of running streams in summer. A distance to the south of a hundred miles and two thousand feet of lesser altitude would have rid this wilderness of its verdant freshness. Like the vast ranges below, much of which was now tilled into wheat fields, it would have been dry, drab, dusty. Snow still lay in streaks in the high ravines, tempering the warm winds that blew from the west.

Blanding's camp of riders was situated on the inside of the west point. That of Marigold Wade and her party lay on the inside too, but a mile or more up the curve, where the rocks began to bulge out of the slope and the pine trees stood in stately groups. A clear rapid stream, smoky-hued with its melted snow, ran along the edge, meandering in meadowlike places and then brawling over stone ribs and rushing across gravel bars, and now and then tarrying in deep blue pools.

Lark Burrell had camped in many places, but never in one so colorful and enchanting as this. Her little tent, whose site she had selected, stood up the gentle slope a dozen rods or more from the cluster of others. It was on the edge of a tiny, level bench, back of which reared a huge gray-lichened rock. A bubbling spring burst from under the green moss and babbled away in a tiny stream. Violets lifted blue faces from the moss, and sage grew almost to the water. Across the stream stood a mighty pine, spreading-branched, full-foliaged and perfect in its straight symmetry. Beyond this, other pines straggled up the slope. Below Lark's temporary habitation trooped more trees, decreasing in size and number toward the more level ground. Farther down the point began the growth of smaller timber and brush.

It had taken two days to pitch camp and make everything comfortable. Marigold had sprung a surprise on her friends, except Lark, who was in on the secret that most of the idea and all of its execution had emanated from Stanley Weston. The equipment had been hauled in a wagon; the members of the party had ridden out; the chuck wagon and the extra saddle horses had not yet arrived, but were at this hour, mid-afternoon of the second day, visible on the horizon. Lark's keen, educated eyes had been first to make this welcome discovery. They had all slept out in the open the first night, a merry, noisy crowd that toward dawn had suffered acutely from the cold. They had also gone pretty hungry and acclaimed the approaching chuck wagon with whoops of joy.

Lark had put in happy hours this day, despite recurrent pangs, and a return of terrible despair; both ailments she had resignedly concluded were mere symptoms of love. But out in the open she could not be utterly happy.

Stanley had assisted materially in choosing the party. Ellery was the only disappointment, Marigold said. She did not, however, vouchsafe any remarks about the girls, Doris McKean and Evelyn Grange, who were close friends. Lark could not help liking them. The two other girls Lark had not yet become acquainted with. Charlie Fairchild and Coil Bruce were with the party, and Stanley's new foreman, Landy Elm, was the fourth and last. So, considering the jolly crowd and Marigold's subtle change, and especially Stanley's comforting presence, Lark's regrets at coming had begun to ooze away. To be sure, when the wild-horse chasing and trapping started, she was going to be distrustful of herself. But that, according to the latest news, would not be for some time yet. Marigold had let her eagerness rush them all out here days ahead of the great drive. Nobody objected; in fact, they regarded the venture as a picnic.

Lark sat on the grassy bank above the place where the spring poured its clear contents into the brook, which made a meandering curve just there. She sighted trout in the deep water: shadowy, wavering forms she knew well. That was an added delight, and just about all that was needed to make this spot perfect, as far as physical attributes went.

"Oh dear," sighed Lark. "Every thought I have—either good or bad—hinges on *him*."

It was useless to chide herself. She could not control her heart. That mysterious member had developed unruly and outrageous reactions of its own.

The black bulk of the chuck wagon loomed larger out on the sage, and a long string of horses took on a livelier color and shape. Lark's keen eye calculated distance and progress. The horses would reach camp in something over an hour, before dusk.

Long shadows reaching out on the sage began to turn purple. The plain faded out there in hazy obscurity. Behind Lark, to the west, over the sloping, wooded ridge, burned the pure gold of sunset, still too brilliant for her eyes. But she could satisfy her yearning fully in the vast bowl narrowing to the amphitheater and sheering wild, shaggily timbered and blue-veiled, up between the dome-shaped peaks. Lark was used to the naked, stark, desert-like vastness of her southern Idaho; rugged, sublime, gripping, but without warm, intimate softness; lacking fragrance, color and heart-compelling beauty like this.

Pine trees were far from her cabin down there; she could just see the patches of black on the mountains. She made comparisons. Here there was no green, white-frothing river like her beloved Salmon. On the other hand, in Idaho no glorious sage bloomed with opal fire at sunset, such as she marveled at now.

The waning light sustained a sudden up-flashing brilliance, a gold and purple medium so thick and lovely as to appear like an ethereal smoke from a celestial fire. It was the afterglow of sunset. Lark sat there enchanted. For a few moments the mantle burned over the ridge, and then slowly began to change. It faded. And it died like an exquisite spirit of nature, going out of life. Cool dark gray lights followed, creeping in from the west.

9

BEFORE DUSK set in, the chuck wagon rolled up to camp, escorted by a number of saddle horses in charge of two riders. They were hailed with wild shouts from the campers. But when Lark ran down to join them she rather inclined to the conviction that the acclaim was mostly for the chuck wagon.

"Jeff, we're starved to death," cried Marigold to the old cook who had been in the service of the Wades for many years.

"Hurrah! Here are the eats!"

"No more stale sandwiches and pickles!"

"Hot biscuits and gravy now. Oh boy!"

"Hey, Miss Mari," asked Jeff, when he could get a word in. "What kinda outfit is this heah, anyway?"

"We're all starving," shouted someone.

"Wal, we'll throw some grub together in a jiffy," returned the cook. "I'm glad you got a hot fire goin'."

One of the cowboys appeared, throwing nose bags out of the wagon. That was a signal for Lark to run.

"Fill one for me," she called to the cowboy. "I'll feed my horse and hobble him."

Chaps was not to be caught until Lark approached him with the nose bag. Then he became a most willing prisoner. Lark took exception to the way he tossed his nose bag high, for every time he did he spilled some of the grain.

"Put your head down, you fool horse," she commanded. "Rest the bag on the ground. There. I'll have to teach you a lot, Cream Puff." She hobbled his forefeet with a soft cotton rope, and stayed beside him until he had finished his grain. Coil Bruce and the other cowboys were looking after the rest of the horses.

"Reckon this isn't new to you?" said Coil pleasantly to Lark. He had manifested keen awareness of her presence on several occasions.

"What? The company or the horses?" asked Lark with a smile. She liked this lad's face.

"Reckon I mean the horses. I watched you put that hobble on."

"I've a ranch full of horses."

"Wild or broke?"

"Some of them are broke. But they're always running off with the wild bands."

"Wild hosses down your way, Miss Lark?" he asked, with increased interest.

"Droves and bands and herds! Thousands of wild horses," she replied.

"Let me give you a hint," he said in lower tone, so that the other cowboys could not hear. "Keep it to yourself. Hurd Blanding has gone into the business of catching wild horses for the market."

"Outside of Washington?" asked Lark in surprise.

"Anywhere. He aims to make big money. Cowboys have tried this before Blanding, but not on so big a scale. It was easy enough to trap wild horses, if they were plentiful. But moving them was the rub. It's some job to drive a bunch of wild horses, as I'll bet you know. But Blanding hit on this tailing trick and he sure can move them."

"I heard about that tailing. If I know wild horses it's as low-down a trick as any cowboy ever thought of," rejoined Lark feelingly.

"Low-down isn't the word, Miss Lark. It's hideous. I was with Blanding on that drive he made some time ago. No more for me! I sure fell out with Blanding over that. The was he does the trick is this: They rope a couple of horses—of course after they're trapped—and throw them close together; then they tie the head of one to the tail of another."

"How close together?"

"Well, they wasn't particular. The idea was to rustle. They didn't care how one horse kicked or dragged the other, so long as they kept them together, and moved them quick. Miss Lark, you're going to see red!"

"How do you know?"

"I reckon you love wild horses. Don't you?"

"Yes. I'm seeing red now."

"Landy Elm hates the trick, too," went on Bruce confidentially. "I heard him say that he'd never let Blanding drive the Sage Hill range. Next time Blanding will get more'n the slam in the jaw Stanley Weston gave him over—"

A step checked Bruce's speech. Marigold had approached from behind. She was leading a black horse.

"What's that you're saying, Coil?" she inquired, almost sharply.

"Aw, nothing much, Miss Wade. It—I—was just talking—"

"So I overheard. You said, 'Next time Blanding will get more than the slam in the jaw Stanley Weston gave him.' Explain, please."

Bruce suddenly recovered from his confusion and faced her. "I said that, yes. We were talking about wild horses. I told Miss Lark that Landy Elm wouldn't let Blanding drive Sage Hill range. And then I went on to say that about Blanding getting more'n a slam on the jaw."

"So that's it, Coil. But I'm sure you could find more interesting gossip for Miss Burrell," returned Marigold curtly. "Please look after my horse. But don't let anyone hobble him."

Lark ran after Marigold, to slip a hand through her arm. "Don't be angry with Coil, cousin. It was my fault."

"I'm not angry with *him*," replied Marigold. "Blanding talks too much. I'm finding that out late in the day. But no matter—Stan shouldn't have hit him. It's created gossip. . . . I'm afraid he's got too much fighting spirit. He always used to be slugging somebody. And they always had to carry the unfortunate fellow out!"

As they approached the campfire, Stanley encountered them, ax in hand. He made a lithe, superb figure in his rough garments and boots.

"Are you both happy?" he said, resting upon the ax and looking down upon them.

"Lark is," replied Marigold, as with Lark still on her arm she went closer to Stanley. "I'd like a word with you, Stanley. I overheard Coil telling Lark about your fight with Hurd Blanding. I taxed Coil about it."

"Well, what of it? I told you," said Stanley, his fine dark eyes, suddenly losing genial light, steady upon Marigold's.

"Yes, but it's made a lot of nasty talk."

"Since when are you concerned with talk?" asked Stanley icily.

"I get you," retorted Marigold furiously. "In other words, if I hadn't been friendly with Blanding—"

"Let's not go into that again, Marigold," Stanley interrupted her. "And this certainly must bore Lark, if it doesn't embarrass her."

Lark felt Marigold stiffen, though she made no further response. Turning her back, she walked away, leaving Lark standing perturbed and miserable before Stanley.

"Oh, Stanley, I'm sorry for her," she whispered. "She sees now—what her willfulness has led to."

"I'm sorry, too, Lark. But I'm more afraid. . . . Run along now. Here come the boys."

At that juncture Jeff let out a stentorian yell: *"All tenderfeet an' sech, come an' get it!"*

There was a wild scramble, punctuated by shrieks of

girls and merry voices of boys. Lark took her time getting there. Two bright lanterns shed a circle of light in the center of the camp, marking Jeff's quarters. A wide canvas fly had been strung up high, under the center of which stood a long table with benches of equal length on each side. Seats had also been built at the ends, the head for Marigold and the foot for Stanley. The girls sat on one side and the boys on the other.

"Where's my place?" asked Lark, when she arrived.

"Any old place," replied somebody.

"Here's room over here," offered another.

"Here, Lark, beside me," called Evelyn Grange, who sat next to the end of the bench. "If you fall off it'll be in Stan's lap."

Stanley had just taken his place when Lark slipped over the bench. Somebody called for Marigold.

"Hey, Marigold," screamed one of the other girls. "The gobblers are on the job."

"I'm coming," replied Marigold, from her tent. And presently she appeared in the circle of light, to take her place at the head of the table. She showed no sign of undue excitement, save perhaps in the dark brilliance of her eyes. "Don't wait on ceremony, kids. Just pitch in."

And so they did. Lark, used to camping out on the range with little food, marveled at this bounteous repast. After that, conversation was fragmentary. This was the first real meal in two days.

An hour later a main campfire, situated under the pines where Stanley's tent had been pitched, drew all to its cheerful, crackling warmth, for the air had grown piercingly cold. The wind off the heights held a keen edge of snow. The girls appeared in coats and sweaters.

"Hey there, you," called Stanley to someone who was bringing camp chairs. "Nothing doing with them round my fire. You all sit on a log or one of these rocks I've so generously arranged."

"This is marvelous," spoke up Doris McKean, a pretty slip of a girl, with blond hair. "Marigold was wonderful to give us this treat."

"Sure. But we'll freeze to death away from the camp-fire," returned another.

"We've got a million blankets. Get some from the store tent," said Marigold.

They were sitting and standing around the fire, all pleasantly attentive to the heat, when Stanley's young foreman joined them.

"Gettin' nippy," he remarked, extending lean red hands over the blazing logs. "I reckon it'll snow on us."

"Had your supper?" asked Stanley.

"I guess I had 'most two suppers."

"What's the news from the other camp?"

"Lots of news," replied Elm. "We got here ahead of the drive. Blanding's got about twenty cowboys and a whole tribe of Indians. Has to feed them and it sure riles him the way they eat. They're building wings for the trap now. Got four miles done. Cutting all the brush in the country."

"Where's the trap going to be, Landy?"

"Not so far, straightaway. Blanding aims to drive for several days, so I hear. He'll start the Indians around to the west some forty miles and ease the wild horses around toward this valley. They're not to chase the horses or scare them. Just move them along day by day. Then when he gets a big bunch between these two ridges he'll drive them up the valley to the notch. There the trap will be ready. It's a natural trap, shaped like a triangle, with only one place where they'll have to build a fence."

"I've been there fishing. Rocky walls. Stream coming down. Heavy brush on one slope," said Stanley.

"Reckon that's it. I've never been there myself. It must be some trap. Blanding expects to round up five thousand horses there."

"Oh, he's out of his head!" exclaimed Stanley incredulously. "There are plenty of horses, of course, but he couldn't handle that number."

"It does seem incredible," admitted Elm.

"Landy, is my brother over there at Blanding's camp?" interposed Marigold.

"Yes. He rode in today, so I heard."

"But I thought El had fallen out with Blanding."

"Must have made up. They were as thick as thieves. Ellery sure had a good laugh when Blanding ordered me out of his camp."

"What'd you say, Landy?" asked Stanley, with increasing interest.

"Well, I told him the range was free and that he could go to hell."

"That's bearding the lion in his den. What then?"

"I hate to tell you, boss," admitted Landy with a laugh.

"Go on. We want to hear."

"Sure . . . I'm sorry to tell you Blanding pulled a gun on me and drove me out."

"You don't say!"

"I do say. Ellery and some of the others remonstrated with Blanding. But he was sure sore. And I beat it."

"Anything more?"

"Yes. I'd mounted my horse and was leaving when he yelled: 'Tell Weston I won't have any of his *male* outfit butting in here, but if his *females* can't get enough entertainment over there at his camp, they sure can get it here. . . .' Those were his exact words, boss. They made me pretty hot under the collar."

A blank silence ensued. Lark noted how Stanley started, and then turned his back to the fire.

"Landy, did my brother stand for that?" inquired Marigold furiously.

"No, he didn't. I heard him just as plainly. He roared: 'Hurd, that's no way to talk. You forget that is my sister's party, not Weston's.' 'Aw, I forgot nothing,' Blanding rapped back at him. 'If you don't like it you know what you can do!' Ellery was cussing when I rode out of earshot."

"Stanley, that crazy cowboy is getting pretty tough," spoke up Evelyn Grange with scorn.

Other rather cold opinions were expressed, but Stanley remained silent.

"Girls, Hurd must have—been drunk," expostulated Marigold, her voice trembling. "There's no other excuse. I'm sorry. It's my fault. Frankly I—I've been too—too nice to Blanding."

"Never mind, Marigold," said Doris McKean. "Don't be upset about it. There's nothing much that you can do."

No more was said on that subject. Gradually the restraint slackened, and presently merriment once more held sway around the campfire. Lark was the first to break away.

"Good night, everybody," she called.

Some of them made gay sallies that Lark answered in a similar vein with: "Early to bed, early to rise, you know."

"I couldn't go to bed this early even for all that," laughed one of them.

"Lark, I'll escort you to your canvas domicile," offered Stanley.

He joined her and they walked in silence until they had gone far past the circle of campfire light, when he spoke: "Lark, our coming out here was a mistake. I told Marigold so. But she would come."

"Stanley, I wouldn't back out now. You stay," replied Lark.

"It might lead to a fight."

"Not if we all keep away from that—that Blanding's camp."

"Maybe. I'm sorry El Wade went back to Blanding. I wasted my breath on El. He's as weak as water."

They arrived at Lark's tent. "Shall I bring you another blanket?" asked Stanley.

"No, thanks. I'll be snug and warm."

"Have you a candle?"

"Me? Stanley, you forget I'm an Idaho cowgirl."

"I don't forget anything about you. But you're not that."

"Hardly," replied Lark with a titter. "I possess only one cow."

There appeared nothing for him to do, or for him to say, yet he lingered. In the starlight his face looked sad.

"Stanley, you're unhappy," she said impulsively. Always, emotion governed Lark. She put a hand on his.

"Child, could you expect me to be ecstatic?" he asked, fastening piercing eyes upon her.

"But you—you must make up with Marigold," faltered

Lark, her courage not so great as her sympathy. "Everything will be all right."

"Will it?"

"Stanley!"

"It will not," he said bitterly. "Oh, Lark, either you're stupid—or not on the level."

"Stupid, surely. But not that other—if it means dishonest."

"I don't mean dishonest. I mean you're not telling me what you might."

Lark trembled with a fear that she divined what he was driving at, and she was about to change the subject when he released her hand, and grasping her by the shoulders he bent low, while he shook her.

"Don't you know Marigold is deceiving me?" he demanded. "She told me she'd flirted with Blanding—but she didn't tell all."

"Why—Stanley—"

"Don't you *know* she's too—too thick with this damned Blanding? . . . Agh! It makes me sick—sick to speak my thought aloud. But don't you know that?"

"What is the reason you ask me?"

"Because you're different. You don't belong to this crowd. You could see right through Marigold Wade."

"Stanley, if I could—and there was anything to—to hurt you—I'd never tell."

"Well, Lark Burrell, I could stand your being just a little less what you are—if it'd help me. But you'd stand behind her. That's the woman of it."

"Hush, Stanley, you are saying what you'll be sorry for," whispered Lark, as he released her. "Marigold spoke up bravely, didn't she? She said she was to blame. Oh, she's game."

"Yes. And if she didn't betray something to you, then she did to me."

"Stanley, you must not think like that," implored Lark. "Marigold has only been thoughtless—vain—indiscreet enough to regret it. *All* those girls fell for Blanding. I heard them say so. He is handsome, and somehow compelling. So don't be hard on Marigold."

"I'd not mind being hard. But I hate the idea of being suspicious—unjust. It was what Blanding taunted me with that bothered me. I have reason to be jealous of him. By heaven, I have!"

"He's only a boaster. What do you care what he said?"

She was wearing him down, making him ashamed, strengthening his faith.

"She must be—all right still—or a girl like you couldn't love her," he burst out hoarsely. "You couldn't. And you do, don't you, Lark?"

"Yes, I love her," replied Lark, feeling her lips stiffen, though that was no lie. Nevertheless she wondered.

"Listen," he began swiftly, thrusting a hand through his hair. "The other night I raised a row with Marigold about her conduct. She was so surprised—and sort of fascinated, you know, until we got home, and then she got angry. She swore at me. We had the worst scrap we ever had. Even then I didn't get it all out. She'd probably have torn out my hair. As it was, when I objected to any more of Blanding's attentions to her, why darned if she didn't laugh in my face. You see, we'd had an understanding. She looked me square in the eyes and laughed. I left then, and slammed the door in my rage. But I gave in to her—and now it's worse."

"Stanley," whispered Lark, now forced to think of her weakening self. "If there *had* been anything—serious—Marigold would have told you. . . . Believe me, Stanley. She's that kind of a girl."

"Lark, how wonderful you are!" he cried, wringing her hands. "You can't imagine what a mess I'm in. You're almost convincing me."

He made as if to kiss her; then, catching himself in time, he rushed away into the darkness.

Lark stumbled into her tent, and on her knees she tied the flaps with her fingers all thumbs. When she got into bed, to pull the blankets up over her, it was none too soon.

She lay there panting. Her heart was so oppressed that it hindered breathing. Stanley's manifest intent was enough to rob Lark of every vestige of strength. She had been reduced to a quivering little mass of nerves. What would happen if Stanley actually were to forget himself and kiss her? No longer could she answer for herself! It was an astounding, ungovernable yearning. The time when she would have been infuriated had passed! And sooner or later he would do it. She felt that. She could not control herself. The longing to save him pain and to be loyal to Marigold had caused her to approach falsehood. For in her heart she now realized something was terribly wrong. Stanley had swept her off her feet with his passionate confidence in her. Why had he told her?

Lark thought about going back to her ranch in Idaho. It might save her from catastrophe, but not Stanley or Marigold. And if she could only keep her secret, what did it matter how she suffered? But could she keep it? She had no more faith in herself. On the other hand, outside of her pride, what did it matter if she did betray herself? It was far better for her to stay on here as long as possible, or until there was no need of her, and then go home. The loneliness of Salmon River Ranch came to her like a soothing wave. Yes, she would return. And meanwhile, with that in mind, she ought to earn some money.

This decision wrested Lark out of her conflict. Less weighty and newer aspects of the situation occupied her. This wild-horse drive held a hideous fascination for her. To see it through had underneath it a curious, wondering hope to see it fail! She meant to ride all over the country and make deductions and conclusions herself.

The wind shook her little tent, bringing back the feeling of the open and the wild. This Washington country had its charm. The big pine that spread its branches over her sang to her in tones familiar to her since childhood.

The hour was late and the air that had free access to her canvas abode was piercingly cold. It was well that she had provided a number of blankets. While she reached for the extra ones and spread them over her bed she heard another familiar wild sound. Yelp of a coyote! Then an answer! The wail, the bark, the whine thrilled her through and through.

She listened for a long time, and once, far away, the

coyotes yelped again. Then, when she was about to fall asleep, from the ridge top back of her tent rose the wild, deep baying moan of a prairie wolf. That made her jerk. That, still more, was like home. And there flooded over her the old, familiar, childhood notion that she was a lone wolf herself.

10

LARK WAS up at the first rosy flush of dawn. These early hours were worth some sacrifice of comfort and sleep.

The men appeared to be astir. Cowboys were chopping wood for the chuck-wagon fire; Jeff's whistle rang out tunefully; the horses were coming in with their awkward hobble; Stanley was at the moment engaged in the task of fanning last night's embers into a blaze. None of the feminine members of the party were in sight.

Lark had put on her Idaho riding outfit, regardless of what comment she might arouse. She did not feel comfortable in the type of riding clothes that Marigold and her guests affected. Moreover, she had donned a buckskin blouse, beaded and fringed, and shiny from long service.

The water in her pail was frozen solid, or at least so hard that she could not break it. "Gee! Here it is nearly May and winter yet!" said Lark. "It's fine now down on the Salmon."

Lark filled her washbasin at the spring, and that water seemed colder to her than melted ice. She was not overlong at her ablutions. Then with fingers stinging she raced for the fire.

"Stanley, you old pioneer," was Lark's merry greeting, as she bent to thaw her pink fingers.

"You pretty thing!" declared Stanley enthusiastically.

"Stanley, aren't you teasing?"

"No, I'm not," he retorted, as he emphatically snapped a stick. "Lark, this sort of life really suits you. You look radiant, believe me. These other girls can't compare with you."

"Thanks, Stanley. But you embarrass me," returned Lark, bold in her newly won independence. "What shall I do if at the last minute at night you—you frighten me—and the very first thing in the morning flatter me?"

"God only knows!" ejaculated Stanley gloomily. "But I may as well confess that I'm crazy about you."

He arose to stride off for more wood, leaving Lark in precisely the same state as on that last moment the night before. Presently she recovered. She thought she understood him. She warmed her buckskin gloves over the fire.

Upon Stanley's return with an armload of wood, Lark informed him that she meant to ride all over the place.

"What you mean, place?" he growled. "Around camp?"

"No. Over the whole country."

"You are not going to do anything of the kind," he said emphatically.

"Oh, but I am. I love to ride, as you know. And I don't imagine Marigold and her friends will care to ride so far. I want to see the country from high up. To watch for wild horses! Did you fetch your glasses?"

He nodded, and deposited the wood on one side.

"I'll borrow them. Then I want to see the building of this fence, and the trap, and everything."

"But, Lark, you can't ride around alone."

"Why can't I?" she asked belligerently.

"Don't ask foolish questions."

"I ride alone all over the range at home."

"That's different. It's wild down there."

"Of course it's wild. Enough for rustlers. They've kept me poor for years!"

"Rustlers! You never told me that!" ejaculated Stanley. "Lark, you don't mean to tell me you ride around alone where there're outlaws?"

"I've had to. Been chased more than once, too, Stanley. I always pack a rifle on my saddle."

"Can you shoot?" he asked dubiously.

"I've a notion I can beat you," she replied.

"You wouldn't have to be so good. How about a small gun—a revolver?"

"I can handle one."

"Well, I'll let you have one, and a belt. Daresay we can cut it to fit you. But, Lark, I'm in no mind to let you ride all over alone, even if you pack a gun."

"Then you'll have to go with me," she returned demurely, gazing down at the fire. It did not matter, because she did not trust herself anyhow.

He gave a short laugh. "That'd be perfectly delightful. But unfortunately I can't do it. I'll manage an afternoon now and then. What do you suppose Marigold and her friends would think, not to say the cowboys, if you and I rode off every day alone? They'd laugh and think—I don't know what. They'd say I was infatuated with you —which probably wouldn't be so far wrong."

"Very well, Stanley. You will have to get somebody to ride with me," rejoined Lark cheerfully.

"One of these cowboys!"

"I suppose. Coil Bruce is nice. And I like Landy very much."

"Oh, you do. Humph. Lark, they're both decent boys. I wouldn't be afraid to trust them. But the trouble is— they'll both fall in love with you in just one day. I'm not so sure but what Coil isn't already."

"What's wrong with that?"

"Lark Burrell, I believe you've got a little devil in you somewhere."

"I hope so. I sure don't want to be a perfect angel."

"There's no great danger of that," he said dryly.

"Stanley, if you're going to take care of me, as you claimed Saturday night, you'll have to run some risks."

"Make the risk past and present tense, Miss Burrell," he retorted in no uncertain tone.

"Oh, have I—offended you?"

"I am perfectly furious with you," he declared, striding away.

But Lark did not believe this. She put on her gloves

and hurrying over to the chuck wagon asked for a nose bag and grain. She had seen quite a little of the weather-beaten Jeff, enough to grasp that they would be friends.

"Mornin', Miss Lark. You're shore up betimes. What you want grain for? You can't eat oats. Reckon you mean coffee?"

"Jeff, I want to feed my horse, of course."

"Ketch him an' feed him all by yourself?" asked Jeff, his wrinkled face expressing real or pretended astonishment.

"Yes. I hobbled him last night. I'm quite capable of roping him, if he gets frisky on me."

"Wal, my eyes are slow. I didn't see thet outfit you've got on. Reckon you're so all-fired pretty thet I didn't see nothin' but your face. Miss Lark, you can have anythin' you want out of this wagon, day or night, early or late."

Lark did not need to be told that she had made a friend. According to Marigold's talk, old Jeff was a wonderful cook, but cranky and very methodical in his ways. To be late for a meal was an unpardonable sin. To ask for food at any other time still worse!

"Thank you, Jeff," replied Lark. "I just knew we'd get along."

"Lordy, I wish I was about forty years younger," he replied. With bag and grain Lark went to look for Chaps. She found him, presently, among the straggling horses. When she called he lifted his head; however, he would not come. Lark went closer and tried again. But not until some of the other horses, particularly Stanley's black, made for Lark did Chaps show any interest. Finally he saw the nose bag and then came in a pounding plunge, as fast as his hobbles would permit.

"Just for that, I'll feed Blackie first," said Lark, and slipped the nose bag on Stanley's horse. Then she ran back for another. This time she encountered Coil Bruce, who looked at her in a way to recall Stanley's prophecy. He greeted her, and sorted out a new, clean nose bag, which he filled.

"That's too much grain," protested Lark.

"Lovely mornin' for a ride, Miss Lark," he said, and it was no casual remark.

"Isn't it?" And receiving the grain from him she tripped away to where Chaps was trying to get his nose into Blackie's bag. This time Lark made Chaps follow her to her tent before she would give him his feed. Then she slipped his hobbles. She had her saddle, blanket, bridle, spurs and other things stowed away beside her tent, covered with a slicker. She now got out a currycomb and brush, which she began to use on Chaps. His mane and tail were full of burrs. While she worked she talked to him, following a habit which she had acquired as a child, when she had few companions but animals.

"Lark, here's the gun and belt," said Stanley, coming up. "I didn't cut the belt. You see, never having had my arm around you, I don't know just how slim you are."

"Not so very slim, Stanley," she replied, turning.

"Let me see," he said, and slipped the belt round her waist. He pulled it tight, and almost toppled her over against him. "All right. The last hole will do. I'll say you're slim. I could span your waist with my two hands. . . . Now I'll cut it here—and trim the end—like this. . . . There you are. The belt is half full of shells, as you can see, and the gun loaded. Are you sure you know guns?"

"Some guns. This looks rather like a toy to me. . . . How pretty and light! I don't feel it at all. If it's a single-action, I'm all right."

"No, it's double-action. A self-cocker. See here." And he broke out the cylinder, extracted the shells, of which there were five, and snapping the gun together he demonstrated its use. "Now let me see you do that."

She handled the gun for him.

"No tenderfoot about you, Lark. When you reload it, keep the hammer on the empty chamber. . . . Say, I saw Coil making faces at you already."

"My, what eyes you have! He did say it'd be a lovely morning to go riding."

"Well, I hate to dash his hopes. We'll ride together this morning."

"All right, boss. I'm raring to go."

"Not a one of the other girls up," he remarked significantly.

"I'll get Jeff to help," replied Lark, laughing gleefully.

"Say, that's a great idea, Lark. And don't lose any time about it."

Lark picked out an opportune moment, and waylaying Jeff as he came with buckets for water she propounded a play which brought a grin to his face. Not long afterward the cool silence of the sunrise was murdered by a tremendous din. Jeff and two cowboys were beating huge dishpans.

Stanley threw up his hands. Then he yelled at the top of his lungs, *"Fire! Indians!"*

Marigold's tent shook. A lovely tousled head protruded from between the flaps. "What in the devil are you up to?" she screamed.

"Sunup!" called Stanley. "Roll out, everybody. There's hot water. Breakfast in fifteen minutes."

"Stan, you'd never have had the nerve yourself," declared Marigold. "I'll bet a million that my little cousin is at the bottom of it."

Other disheveled heads appeared from other tents.

"Oh, where are they?" gasped Doris McKean.

During the next half hour, one by one the feminine contingent appeared, making a beeline for the fire, and Marigold was the last.

"What's the idea?" she shrilled, as she buttoned a red coat round her. "It's only seven o'clock!"

"Lark and I were the first up, so we inaugurated early rising for the rest of you," declared Stanley.

"I knew it. Lark's inspiration and your execution. Well, my middle name's game," replied Marigold, as she pinched Lark's cheek. "Good morning, cousin . . . Look at her, girls. Did you ever see any creature more calculated to upset the equilibrium—"

"Come to the festal board!" bawled Jeff.

An hour later the party were mounted and riding up the slope back of camp.

The morning, now that the sun had tempered the cold,

was something to invigorate the most phlegmatic. A glorious brightness pervaded the atmosphere. It shone on the sage. It brought out the cold, pure white of snow in the high crevices. A steely gray vied with the black and green timber on the ridges.

Lark's desert-practiced eye soon made out a long, dark, uneven line of cut trees and brush, extending across the valley in a diagonal slant toward the other point. This was the fence erected by the wild-horse hunters. It ran from Blanding's camp several miles beyond the opposite point, out into the sage. Wild horses working down the plain would be turned inward by that fence.

"They're cutting on the other side of that point," explained Stanley. "Not such a long haul. They aim to run the fence several miles farther out."

Various comments were made. Lark had nothing to say, but she felt a great deal. Her sharp eyes had made out a string of riders dragging brush across the sage, and beyond them, far out in the gray, a multitude of tiny specks that she knew to be wild horses. Someone asked Landy if Blanding's first drive had been on this side of the mountain, and was answered in the negative. Lark had figured that out for herself.

They rode three miles or less up the gradually ascending ridge, from which the view increased in scope and impressiveness. Far north, over the slope of Horse Heaven Hill, showed the dark wavering line of another mountain range. Kettle Mountains, Landy called them, and they lay across the great river.

"Reckon that hole down there is Blanding's trap," said Landy Elm.

"It is. My word! Nature and the devil have connived with Mr. Blanding," declared Stanley.

"Landy, please explain this trap," suggested Marigold, nervously impatient. "I don't know what to look for."

"Look where the level valley begins to converge," began Elm, pointing far out. "There's the deceit of this place. You see how the ridge on each side slowly runs in to meet at the notch up here. At the same time the sides of the ridge get rough. They couldn't be climbed. Horses runnin' fast an' scared wouldn't even try. They'd sweep into the notch. That's where the slopes almost meet. It's a wide gateway. It's like the neck of the bottle openin' out on the inside. Well, you all see that big hole, walled in on three sides, and with a brushy bank on the fourth. Blanding will throw a fence across there. An' another fence across the openin', leavin' space for gates. They'll chase the horses in there an' shut 'em in. Plenty of grass an' water. Blanding can take his time ropin' an' tailin' them."

"That's plain as the nose on your face, Landy," declared Stanley. "But it's fifty miles to the cattle yards, where the horses have to be loaded on freight trains."

"That's nothin', after they get the horses tailed. They'll run 'em in to the railroad in less'n a day. They've done it already."

"Wild horses? Tied head and tail!"

"It shore is a bloody mess. But it can be done."

Lark rode a little farther on, the better to see. This kite-shaped flat below, consisting of perhaps fifty acres of grassy level, watered by a stream that entered in a white cascade through the apex, had high unscalable walls round more than three-quarters of its circumference. The remaining boundary, which was a break in the wall, could be fenced with a little labor by many hands. The gate presented the only problem to Lark. There had to be room for an onslaught of wild horses. The place indeed was a diabolical trap.

"Let's go down," suggested somebody. "It's pretty down there."

No other member of the party had voiced that virtue of the enclosure below; and now it struck Lark suddenly, adding more to the emotion within.

There was no trail; however, the descent appeared gradual and the way not long. The riders struck out in single file to follow Landy Elm. Lark, loath to set foot in what would soon become a trap for high-spirited wild horses, was the last to leave. Likewise she was the last to discover that the bulge of the ridge slope had hidden a man-made barricade below the line of brush where she had calculated Blanding would fence the break. Trees of sapling size had been cut and piled in a thick hedge all along the edge of the enclosure, on that weak side. Lark rode to the end, close to where the stream dashed singingly over the jumbled boulders. It was perfectly natural for her to think of ways and means by which the wild horses could escape. They could not climb the waterfall, nor any of the walls. The fence presented a flimsy barrier so far as actual stability was concerned. But all that was necessary to turn wild horses was merely something they did not think they could surmount. A desperate stallion might attempt to leap the fence, which in most places had snags and spikes enough to lacerate him cruelly, if not kill him outright. Whole trees had been dragged down the slope, and these in many instances served as piers to which could be anchored saplings and branches and lighter brush.

The aperture through which Marigold's party had ridden into the trap had no gate yet, but piles of trimmed poles lay on the ground ready to be used.

"What do you say to our taking a stand up on that wall when Blanding's outfit drives the horses in?" suggested Stanley.

"I'm not anxious to," replied Marigold.

Her friends singly and in unison were not of her mind, and they besought her until she cried: "Mercy! If that's the way you feel, we'll come. . . . Lark, what do you think about this?"

"It is bad," replied Lark simply.

"I'll tell you what," suggested Stanley. "Tonight round the campfire let's have a talk about the relative merits and demerits of wild horses."

"Heavens, Stanley!" laughed Marigold.

"I think it's some idea," declared Evelyn Grange.

"What do we know about wild horses?"

"That's just it. We don't. But the cowboys do and surely Lark knows something about them," replied Stanley. "And it's up to us to learn."

They sat their mounts and argued. Lark again rode over the ground. She was aware of being repelled yet fascinated by this project of Blanding's. She was wholly on the side of the wild horses. This second time she bent scrutinizing and photographic eyes upon that brush fence without any intent other than bitter curiosity. But the act was productive. It sent scintillating thoughts through her brain. Some of the brush and wood was green; most of it was dry; it had been packed thick and high; its length was perhaps two hundred yards; and it would burn like tinder. Suppose someone who loved wild horses happened to burn the fence!

The idea neither surprised nor shocked Lark Burrell. It just flashed into her mind. Over and over she turned it. She wished there was a cowboy in the party who would do just that thing. She could almost love him! She would have been able to, if she had not given all the love in her being to Stanley Weston. She wondered if he would do it.

The idea not only stayed with Lark, but it grew. Better to let Blanding make the drive, and then, late that night, when the tired riders were all locked in slumber, fire the brush. It would be still more advisable to open the fence, so in case it did not burn the horses could still escape. Then, while Blanding's minions labored to rebuild, the horses would have days to get far away. Not improbably, two such burnings would frustrate the wild-horse raid.

Someone hallooed for Lark to come. The party were riding down into the valley. Lark followed, walking Chaps, to his evident surprise, for he champed his bit. Now she devoted her attention to the lay of the ground along the left side. It was perhaps three miles from Marigold's camp to the site of the trap. This distance presented no obstacle to a rider who might desire to go over it under cover of darkness. Nor would it daunt a girl brought up on the range!

A girl? Here Lark caught herself with a gasp. What was she thinking about? This trend of thought was only a recurrence of an old habit of hers: dreaming of what she would like to do. Many had been the impossible feats of her dreams. She laughed at herself. What would Marigold think, or Stanley, if they could be treated to the direction of her mind? It was impossible to anticipate her cousin's opinion, but Stanley would call her a little outlaw.

"Cream Puff, I could do it. *We* could," she whispered. "And oh, wouldn't I love to cheat that Blanding out of his chicken feed!"

The mustang tossed his head, at a touch of spur rather than Lark's words, and broke into a swinging lope. She soon caught up with the party, riding in pairs and groups. Lark went right on, which was a signal for the others to race. At least Marigold let out a pealing trill upon which her friends acted. The going was level and, despite its growth of sage, easy travel for a sure-footed horse. Lark let them catch up with her. Marigold looked wonderful on a horse, but she was no cowgirl in the saddle.

"Come on, my Idaho cousin," cried Marigold challengingly.

Then Lark urged Chaps into a run. She passed Marigold and the other girls as if they had been tied. Stanley hung closest to her, but he, too, lost ground. The cowboys and other riders hung back with the girls, no doubt enjoying the race. With an even start Lark beat Stanley badly in a three-mile race to the long section of Blanding's fence.

Stanley came thundering on, having hard work to slow down his spirited black.

"Say, Lark, that was great. I congratulate you," he declared.

"What for?"

"The way you ran away from everyone. Marigold thinks she can ride in rodeos. I've had a deal of trouble keeping her out of them."

"Marigold rides well for a girl who hasn't ridden much," said Lark, meaning to be complimentary.

"Ha! Wait till I tell her that!"

The others came in presently, and, when Marigold, rosy and beautiful, with her blond hair flying, arrived to halt her mount, Stanley burst out: "Marigold, I see you also ran. Listen to this. Lark says you ride well for a girl who hasn't ridden much."

Marigold's eyes grew round and big, while her friends laughed delightedly.

"Cousin, you know what I mean," Lark hastened to say. "For a girl who's not ridden the range like I have."

"Lark Burrell, don't make excuses for me," cried Marigold. "I thought I was good. But, heavens, I can't compare with you. Lark, you're just marvelous on a horse. I nearly fell off at the sight of you. And didn't you make Chaps run? . . . Stanley, weren't you surprised?"

"Not at all. I've raced Lark before," he returned, laughing.

"Coil and Landy—you're cowboys," went on Marigold, eager to win encomiums for Lark. "What do you think of Lark?"

Coil was visibly confused. "I—I sure think Miss Lark's a wonderful girl—I—I mean rider."

But Landy drawled, with a twinkle in his keen hazel eyes, "She can ride for me."

Stanley interposed with cool heartiness, "I may offer her a job someday."

Marigold flashed a lightning-swift glance at Stanley, who apparently did not catch it, or see any significance in it.

"Where do we ride from here?" called one of the girls.

"Let's go," urged Marigold.

Lark dropped to the rear again, where Coil Bruce joined her. "Can I ride along with you?"

"Surely. But I warn you I'm a poor partner for a horse-back ride."

"Why so? You can ride!"

"Oh, I'm all right in a race. But otherwise I'm no good. I just can't talk while riding."

"If you ask me, I'd say you didn't need to," he returned boldly, and that marked Bruce's definite change of attitude.

He was a likable cowboy and amused Lark. It interested her, too, that once Stanley had turned round to see Bruce with her, he kept looking back at intervals. Lark pondered upon it and came to the conclusion that Stanley did not care to have any of these Wadestown young men pay her attention. But why? Lark began to feel dubious about the big-brother relation. She had never had a brother and felt herself at a loss there; nevertheless, Stanley's attitude did not fit her conception of fraternal relationship. And she was warmly, deeply conscious that Stanley's peculiar reaction was not only welcome to her, but most disturbing and thought-provoking.

The brush fence and the wild-horse drive, however, took precedence over any other thoughts in Lark's mind for the time being.

This drift fence must now be more than six miles long, Lark calculated. It had been built in the same way and out of the same brush as the shorter barrier back in the trap. Either weeks of labor or many hands on the job had been necessary to make such a showing. The party, headed by Stanley and Marigold, were riding along the first half of the fence, toward where it joined the point at Blanding's camp. Soon the leaders turned away, evidently not desiring to approach any farther.

Lark grew tormented again by the recurring and persistent idea of how easily these barriers could be destroyed by fire. She was annoyed with that unknown, erratic side of herself, and suspicious of it.

"Let's ride close to Blanding's camp," she suggested to Bruce.

"Stanley told us to keep away from there," he replied.

"Are you afraid of him?"

"Afraid! No, indeed. Stanley's the best fellow in the world. But he's runnin' this camp business. And he won't like it."

"Let's try and see what he does."

Bruce was plainly worried, but he rode along with her. It was not many minutes before Stanley discovered their deflection and let out a ringing call.

"There," said Coil.

"Didn't take him long," replied Lark, smiling guiltily and turning Chaps away from the fence. Presently Lark became aware of a tall man in shirt sleeves walking down to where the sage met the gentle slope. The distance was considerable, but she could see well enough to believe she recognized Blanding.

"Big outfit over there," Coil was saying. "See Blanding himself down by the rocks to take a look at us. He's got a glass on you."

Lark took no further notice. "Do you know Blanding well?" she asked.

"I've worked under him a couple of years."

"Is he a real cowman?"

"Cowman? Naw. I could run an outfit myself better than Blanding," replied Coil, with force unusual for him.

"How'd it come he was boss of the Wade outfit?"

"Blanding blew into Wadestown with a couple of other men. They went broke and the others left. He'd gotten acquainted and he hung around. Ellery Wade got to know him and Miss Marigold took him up. And of course everybody did then. He went to Mr. Wade, so they say, and got the job."

"Coil, do you remember the first time I came out to the barn?" asked Lark earnestly. "You took me for a boy. You were pretty sassy. You—"

"Aw, I wasn't just that," interrupted Bruce, surprised into rapture at her use of his first name.

"Never mind that. I sat down to wait until one of you got ready to fetch me a horse. You were throwing dice. Blanding was winning, so it seemed. And either you or the other cowboy, Red, said Blanding was as lucky at dice as he was at love. Or some such talk. Do you remember?"

"I guess. Somethin' like," replied Coil. "An' Hurd said it wasn't luck. I reckon it's not, Miss Lark. He's a regular ladykiller. When he shoved Red and me out of it we were sure he would come bobbin' up to go ridin' with you. But he didn't. He was as black as thunder and sore as a pup. Maybe that didn't just tickle Red and me!"

Lark weighed this opportunity cautiously. She did not regard her prompting of Bruce as disloyalty to Marigold. But that scene in the living room haunted her. Marigold's light version of it had ceased to be unquestionable. This cowboy, however, who was a nice boy and belonged to a good family in Wadestown, might clarify the murk in Lark's mind. He might, by a few chance words, help to re-establish Marigold on a tottering throne; he might, too, Lark thought dismayingly, make some inadvertent or unwitting remark which would only add fuel to the fires of distrust. Lark decided not to induce Coil to make any more confidences. But no sooner had she made this decision than she divined it was too late.

"Lark," began Coil frankly, though his tan cheek reddened. "Blanding told me he had made a play for you—in the stall that—day—and you'd turned him down."

"Made a play?" inquired Lark puzzled.

"Yes. Got fresh. To be right out with it—he tried to hug and kiss you—and see how far he could go. He laughed about it. And he said to me, 'Coil, there's once I got the icy stare. But you might get away with it if you tackle it slow! . . .' I cussed him good. And I told him you was not that kind of a girl."

Lark stared with open mouth at the shamefaced yet eager youth who was thus taking advantage of his opportunity. She warmed to his championship of her, yet so strong was her disgust at the revelation of Blanding's suggestion that she could not find her tongue.

"I've been achin' to tell you this," went on Bruce. "You've guessed how Blanding has lorded it over us cowboys. We seldom get invited anywhere. I've got girl friends who wouldn't look at Hurd Blanding, the same as you wouldn't. But he runs in that crowd, or he did until Stanley slugged him for makin' a hint about Miss Marigold, right before all of Stanley's cowboys. Afterward Stanley fired Howard, and now Howard's tellin' it all over."

"What was the—the hint, Coil?" asked Lark.

"Hal Fletcher told me. He was there and Hal's a truthful fellow. Blanding threw in Stanley's face that he had cause to be jealous."

"Is that the talk going around?" went on Lark faintly.

"That's nothin'. Wait till I—I tell you," choked Bruce, in his growing agitation. "My reason for tellin' you is decent, to my way of thinkin'. You're Marigold's cousin and you're—well, you're more like the Western girls my mother tells about. You might do somethin' to help Stanley. We all think heaps of him. And Marigold is double-crossin' him. We cowboys all know it. But Stanley doesn't. Nobody dares put him wise to what's goin' on. He'd beat anybody half to death. But he ought to know and he's goin' to find out sooner or later. Too late unless you can get around Marigold. No one else could, that's a cinch."

"But why get around Marigold?" asked Lark hopelessly, as Bruce halted impressively.

"Because if you don't she'll be disgraced sure as shootin'," resumed Bruce. "And Stanley will be ruined. Worse, he might kill Blanding."

"Blanding?" echoed Lark weakly. That scene in the living room stood out in a vivid etching of fire on Lark's distracted consciousness.

"Yes, Blanding. He hates Stanley and he's got it on him, Lark. I—I hate to say this. Marigold is sweet and lovely and proud. But she meets Blanding out in the sage. Used to ride two or three times a week with him. Meets him in town. Dances an' drinks openly with him. She's as wild as a March hare."

"Oh, how—dreadful!" whispered Lark huskily.

"It sure is. But I'm glad I got it off my chest. You're the right kind of a girl and maybe you can do somethin'."

"I'll try. Only—what is there to do?"

"Catch her in the act. Aw, now Lark, don't look so sick. This is straight talk. And you're no doll-faced town girl. Catch Marigold! She'll meet Blanding out here—somewhere—sometime. I haven't watched that flaxen-haired lady these six months for nothin'. Catch her and scare her into some sense. Maybe it isn't too late."

Bruce left Lark then and abruptly turned off toward the improvised corral near camp, which they had almost reached. He should have done so sooner, Lark thought with dismay, for there right in her path Stanley had halted his horse and was waiting for her. Fortunately Marigold and the others had ridden on ahead.

Lark tried to pull herself together, and had a few rods in which to do so. How inadequate these were she realized when she looked up to encounter Stanley's piercing eyes.

"Lark, you shouldn't have ridden off—" He checked that admonition. "Say, you're pale. Lark! Has that locoed cowboy been making love to you?"

"I'm afraid he has," replied Lark, leaping at straws.

"I'll call him good and plenty, believe me," declared Stanley.

"Please don't, Stanley. It was my fault. I asked him to ride toward Blanding's camp."

"But I told him not to. And I told you."

"It's not his fault. I insisted. I'm sorry. I won't disobey again. Promise you won't scold Coil?"

"Coil! So it's gotten that far?" he ejaculated fiercely.

"What's—gotten far?" faltered Lark, welcoming anything till she could recover.

"Your friendliness toward that towhead. I had a fight with Marigold about it. Now I'll have one with you."

"Why with Marigold?"

"She said it'd be great if you fell in love with Coil. Such a fine clean boy! Would come into his father's ranch someday! . . . Oh, I was sore. . . . Lark, I'm upset about —well, never mind. But don't *you* fail me. . . . I'm afraid I swore at Marigold. . . . Lark, you're not falling in love —are you?"

"Yes!" cried Lark hysterically, and spurred on ahead.

11

"LOOK HERE, Stan. What do you care if he does?" demanded Marigold.

Stanley, to his chagrin, had spoken his thought aloud, anent his suspicion that Coil Bruce, the conceited cowpuncher, was making love to Lark. Marigold had turned upon him the battery of two penetrating blue eyes. He had to face them. He had to look innocent when he was nothing of the kind. And this situation, which had grown imperceptibly sharper every day for some time, was getting on Stanley's nerves.

"It'd be a fine thing if he did, provided Lark fell in love

with him," went on Marigold. She spoke highly of Coil's family and his prospects.

"Bunk!" exploded Stanley. "Coil may be what you women call a good catch. But not for Lark Burrell."

"Why not for her?" asked his fiancée curiously.

"He—I—oh, hell! . . . Would *you* consider Coil for yourself?"

"For a husband? Heavens! You are getting beyond me, Stan."

"Lark is as good as you, or any of your friends," protested Stanley, and it was on his tongue that she was a great deal better.

"If you mean innocence and all that stuff, she is," returned Marigold scornfully. "But Lark is a country-bred girl and would make the right kind of wife for someone like Coil."

Not to agree with Marigold here was a tactless thing to do, but it was impossible, wherefore Stanley kept silent.

"Stan, are you falling in love with this—this young goddess in blue jeans?" asked Marigold incredulously.

"No," retorted Stanley, sure of his veracity, for the catastrophe was not of the present tense. It had happened.

"Well, you talk damn funny," rejoined Marigold seriously. "If you were at all like any of the other men I know, I'd think you a liar. As it is, all I can say is that you seem rather romantically and absurdly sentimental about my cousin."

"I daresay. You and your dear friends have single-track minds," replied Stanley with sarcasm. "The pursuit of pleasure! But thank God I've more in my head than that. It hasn't occurred to you that Lark is lonelier here than she could have been down in Idaho, where there wasn't anybody. She can't adapt herself to your crowd. She doesn't know how. On the other hand you ought not lay her open to the advances of cowboys."

"So you have become a champion of unsophisticated maidenhood?" inquired Marigold satirically.

"I always was. However, I can't say that you gave me any exercise for my old-fashioned peculiarity."

"Stanley, things are going wrong between us," she answered poignantly.

"No wonder. You've been going your own way."

"That doesn't mean it's hopeless."

"No, Marigold. But you'd better pay some attention to my feelings."

She was silenced, which was an unusual state for Marigold Wade.

"Ride along, darling. I'll wait to have a word with Coil and Lark," Stanley said.

"Very well—darling. But remember what I said: You're riding for a fall," she flung at him, and rode on.

Stanley waited for Lark to come up. Coil had left her to ride up the slope toward the back of the camp. Stanley had it in mind to lecture Lark, but one glance at her distressed face softened as well as frightened him. He did not start off wisely, and thereafter during that short colloquy, he was not himself and must have appeared silly and jealous to Lark. It was certain that his nagging increased her perturbation, and her last choking affirmation crushed him.

Riding over to the corral, Stanley gave his horse to one of the cowboys and sought his tent, where he lay down in a state of despair—furious with Marigold, furious with Lark, furious with himself! For an hour he raged impotently. This hour had been coming and he gave himself up to it.

One result of it was enlightenment. He was ten thousand times more in love with Lark Burrell than he had ever been with Marigold Wade. He felt that he would have succumbed to this passion even if Marigold had not forfeited his respect, and worn thin the fabric of love. He still bore her love, but how pale a ghost of what it once had been! It was the habit of years, something mixed up with school days and family and old ties. It had pity and chivalry and an honest responsibility, a longing to save. But this last seemed futile. He was about ready to give up trying. Marigold was an enigma. She held to the letter of their engagement, if not the spirit; she protested that her love had not changed; but on the evening of their last quarrel she had again put off marriage indefinitely. They were at odds. Stanley had long been easygoing, trusting, patient, hopeful. That had about ended. She had run the whole gamut of sophisticated argument; she had resorted to ridicule, resentment, outraged pride, anger and at last tears. But these had not mended the breach.

There they were. It was a melancholy spectacle. Would this continue after marriage, if Marigold ever did keep her word? If so, it were better that she did not. But he did not feel himself freed. He would see this through, trusting Marigold, hoping that wifehood and motherhood would transform her.

But the state of his heart—that was another matter. He had no control over that. Lark Burrell was the ideal of his dreams from boyhood to manhood. She was the kind of girl he would like to take to his father. But that could never be, even though Marigold failed him. Lark, the simple, lonely, hungry hearted child, had gone to the first young man bold enough to make decent love to her. Stanley would have liked to wring Coil Bruce's neck; nevertheless he was glad it was Coil who had won her. Still, had he? There had been something strange, poignant, violent, mocking in Lark's eyes. There never was any telling about a girl. Stanley pondered. He would corner Lark and tax her about this. But, supposing she got over whatever it had been; he had only to look forward to the same thing, and inevitably more serious, with another man.

Long after lunch hour Stanley emerged from his tent, strengthened only in this—that he must carry on.

The afternoon was hot and the shade of the pines very desirable. Marigold lay asleep in her hammock, one pretty foot and ankle exposed. Two of the other girls were lounging on blankets spread on the ground. Jeff was whistling around his wagon, puttering at camp improvements. Coil and Landy were shoeing a mettlesome horse and not enjoying it. No one else was in sight.

Stanley strode off for a long walk up the slope. He had gotten over his anger at himself and believed a lonely hour on the heights might help him to face his bitter problem.

Once out of sight of camp he forgot it. The pines, the brush, the cactus and sage, the rocks, the clear, green, white-flecked heights, the endless gray expanse below wove their spell around him.

Fully two miles up the slope he found himself in rough country. This was over on the other side of the ridge, facing the east. Rocks had rolled down from the mountain-top in great profusion. Pines had increased in size and number, and spruce had appeared. The sage had thinned out.

He was about to throw himself down in the shade, to rest and think, when a sound startled him. He listened. From the other side of a projecting rock came short, gasping sobs. Could he be hearing right? It was a few rods distant—this high, shelving rock. There was a girl behind it. Stanley divined it could be no one else but Lark.

His first instinct was to depart as noiselessly as he had come, but he was unable to act upon it. After a moment's silence the sobs burst out in a paroxysm. They started the blood back to Stanley's heart. What in the world was the matter with the girl?

He stepped beyond the corner of rock, and glided between it and the spreading spruce foliage into a little insulated nook, half sunny, half shady. On the ground in the center of it lay Lark, face down. She was tearing the grass with her hands. Her coat half covered her dark head, the disheveled, glinting locks of which quivered in unison with the quivering of her slender form.

"Lark!" he called thickly.

She stiffened and lay perfectly still.

"Lark—child—what is it?"

Suddenly she leaped like bent steel released, whirling clear over on her back. All the woe and passion of life convulsed that face.

"*You!*"

"Yes—it's I, Lark," he said huskily.

"Followed—me?" she panted.

"No!"

"Oh, you did—you did!"

"Lark, I swear I didn't," he protested.

"You slip up—on me—here—when I am —alone."

"It was accidental," replied Stanley, hurriedly going down on one knee. "I wanted to be alone myself. And I was coming along back of this rock, working my way through, when I heard something. It was you—sobbing. I just knew it."

"Then—why didn't you—go away?" she wailed.

"Why, Lark, how could I? Leave you alone—way up here?"

"You've only—made it worse." Tears flooded her dilated eyes afresh and coursed down over her wet, reddened cheeks. Her lips trembled. Evidently strength of will and body had ebbed low. She lay limp on her back, her head raised slightly upon her coat, which had crumpled under it.

Stanley took out his handkerchief and wiped her tear-stained face.

"I'm a—baby—you think."

"If I did, it wouldn't matter," he returned soberly, feeling the inevitability of this meeting.

She had not for a moment stopped the low, hard breathing. "Nothing—matters," she cried wildly, and burst out anew, pulling the coat over her face.

"You'll smother," he protested.

"I don't care. . . . Y-you go a-away."

"I won't do anything of the kind. What ails you, Lark?"

"Get out. I t-tell you I c-can't stand *you* here!"

"I'm sorry. You'll have to." And Stanley sat down with his back to the rock. He pulled the coat off her face ,and, taking her by the wrists, he dragged her so close that her shoulders rested upon him. This was not at all what he had intended to do. But he throttled an insane impulse to kiss her wet eyes and red lips.

"Stanley—if—if you say another—word—I'll scream —I'll fight," she threatened, her hands clenched over her breast.

"Go ahead. But first tell me what it's all about. Then maybe you won't want to."

"I want to go—home."

"Back to Idaho?"

"Yes." She sobbed convulsively in his arms, sagging heavily against him.

"Lark, after our ride this morning—when I asked you if you were falling in love—you said yes."

"I—I lied," she cried.

"How so? Just to tease me?"

"No—no! Because I was near crazy."

"That's no reason to lie about such a serious thing. Why did you lie about falling in love?"

"Be-because I—I w-wasn't falling."

"But you said yes."

"Oh, Stanley—won't you go away—leave me here?" she implored.

"Not much. We're going to get at the root of this trouble. And I'd be likely to let you stay here alone? Huh!"

"But you—you don't act like a—a brother—or a father."

"No, I don't. That's true. But I might discover myself in some other capacity."

"You fool—you tease—when my h-heart's breaking."

"I was never more serious in my life, Lark. You've probably got a wrong idea about me. . . . Now explain why you lied to me about falling in love."

"How could I—b-be falling—when I'd fallen—already?"

"Oh—I see," returned Stanley unsteadily. His emotion was a lifting, tremendous thing. "When did you?"

"W-weeks a-ago." She slipped out of his arms enough to sit on the grass beside him, still resting her head on his shoulder. "Lend me your handkerchief." She took it and wiped her eyes. "No use blubbering. It might as well come out. It had to."

"Lark, you're a very remarkable girl. Do I understand that you couldn't be falling in love with Coil because you'd already fallen?"

"Coil! What on earth has *he* to do with it?"

Stanley had difficulty in replying at all, to say nothing of enunciating clearly.

"But—isn't it—Coil?"

"No! No! No! You thickhead! You—you—" She broke off passionately.

"Then—who is this—lucky man?"

The blue heavens were about to fall upon Stanley, he knew. She was silent long moments, while he waited in breathless suspense. Her head still leaned against his shoulder, giving him only part view of her downcast face.

"It is you, Stanley," she said simply, with none of the agitation that had characterized her former speech.

"Me! My God, Lark—what are you saying?" he gasped.

Lark moved out a little to look up at him, and put a hand on his knee.

"Stanley, can you look me in the eyes and say you didn't try to make me love you?"

"Lark, I tried with all my might not to," he declared with strong feeling. "I—I'm engaged to Marigold! What can you think of me?"

"I think you're all that's good and fine and wonderful," she rejoined. "But I wanted to know. . . . It just happened — But Stanley, I never met such a man as you. I was just swept away. It's just as well. Otherwise such a silly girl as I am might have loved a worthless man. But I don't believe I would have."

"Lark, I'm knocked off my feet," said Stanley foolishly.

"But don't feel badly—or sorry. I know nothing can come of it. You're going to marry my cousin. It's a matter of her salvation now. . . . Oh, Stanley, you must make her consent—just as soon as we get back. . . . As for me . . . I sort of feel rid of a terrible hurt. After all, it wasn't shameful. I wouldn't be afraid to tell Marigold. But the dammed-up thing inside of me drove me wild. . . . It's funny, but now I'm glad you found me here."

"If it has helped you, I reckon I'm glad," replied Stanley composedly, in the iron grip he had of himself. When he let go he imagined he would be in an avalanche. That had better be after Lark and he had separated. "But, child, how about you now?"

"I'd thought that all out before today," she replied. "I

must work to earn some money. Then go back to my Salmon River Ranch."

"For good?"

"Forever," she breathed softly.

Stanley looked away from her. For a man who knew he returned her beautiful love in like measure, the natural thing seemed to be to take her in his arms and tell her. No memory of Marigold held him here. Nor even his honor! It was the simplicity of this girl who could confess her love without shame, and who by all hazards must never be made to feel shame. She elevated his soul. She roused him to love beyond the lure of physical possession.

"Home to Idaho," he mused, and thoughts burst like streaking stars in his mind. "But you needn't go soon."

"Perhaps not so soon. It's bearable now. If I can only help Marigold! And I must earn money, Stanley."

"To fix up your ranch? Make it productive?"

"Oh dear no. That would take thousands of dollars," she rejoined wistfully. "I mean enough to live on. We—you know about old Jake—we have a hard time keeping body and soul together. We need food supplies, things to plant, a plow, tools—the leaky old cabin roofed — Oh, there's so much to do. It'll not take a great deal of money."

"How much?"

"Two hundred dollars would do it. I—I could earn that, couldn't I, before next winter? I'll write Jake that I'm coming home in the fall."

"Sure. You could earn that," replied Stanley quietly, while he wanted to yell and tear his hair.

"Could you help me to get a job?"

"Yes. I'll *get* you one, if you'll give me a little time," he said, rapturous plans forming in his mind. The job he meant was that of mistress of Sage Hill Ranch. For he felt now that he could never marry Marigold.

"You've been so kind—so good, Stanley. I'm afraid that accounts—a little—for the damage."

"Tell me about this Idaho ranch of yours. Describe it —ranch, range and all. Can you?"

"You just listen," she replied eloquently, her eyes once more dimmed and sad.

Through simple words then, and feeling that was the well-spring, Lark drew a picture for Stanley.

Batchford was a weather-beaten, old-time range village, far off the railroad. The rough road leading south from there climbed for miles to the top of a divide from which the wild, unfenced, uninhabited south central part of Idaho stretched in a gray vista of range, crossed by a shining river, on to wastes of the lava lands and to the yellow, bare cliffs, to the far sloping hills, and still on and up to the black timber-belted mountains.

Clouds of dust rose beyond the river from moving droves of wild horses.

At the foot of the four-mile hill, from the top of which this magnificent view revealed itself, began the ranch of hundreds of acres of which Lark's father had gotten possession. It was loamy soil. It would stand dry farming, but with irrigation it would blossom into a land of milk and honey. There was a fine brook running through the ranch, but it took money to raise water high enough to flow over that land. There was timber on the extreme east side of the property. Wild horses jumped the rickety old fence to browse on Lark's ten-acre patch of alfalfa. Deer leaped the enclosure round the garden. Coyotes killed the chickens; foxes stole the pigeons; eagles swooped down on the rabbits; wolves and panthers made away with the calves.

Barn and shed and corral had been patched until they could stand no more patching, and little more of the stiff winds and of the snow that fell rarely.

The cabin was big, solid, still strong except for the leaky roof. It had been erected by homsteaders before Burrell's day, and had a living room with a huge open fireplace, and a sleeping room, besides a stone kitchen of later construction. On the flat stone fireplace, quaint Indian designs had been chipped with a rude tool, long years before. Here on the floor was a thick, woolly sheepskin, upon which slept Wixy, the black dog that had come from some unknown place to make his home at the ranch. On the other side of the hearth stood the antique armchair that Burrell's father had brought with him in a wagon train.

Here Lark abruptly ended her description of the home she had left. Her voice had faltered and failed, but she gave no other sign of emotion, except to avert her face.

"You forgot the river and the big trout," prompted Stanley.

"No. But I've told you about them more than once."

"I'll bet I'd love your place," mused Stanley, and there was completed in his mind a resolve to go down into Idaho, when opportunity afforded.

A constraint fell upon them. For Stanley's part he welcomed it. If Lark broke down again, or if she spoke once more in her incredible simplicity of her love for him, Stanley could not answer for the consequences. There was no telling what Lark might say or do. She had never been used to regarding herself as a feminine creature.

"Let's go," suggested Stanley.

"I'd rather stay here alone."

"Nothing doing. It's too far from camp. Suppose, for instance, that Blanding happened upon you way up here. Suppose he jumped off his horse—made a grab for you! . . . Lark, you know he would."

"You don't need to tell me that."

"Well, what would you do?" asked Stanley, sure of her reaction, but desiring to hear her express it.

"I'd hold him up with a gun," she said fiercely, and slipped the revolver he had given her from the pocket of her jeans.

"Ahuh. So you carry it there?"

"Yes. The belt was heavy, and besides—I'd rather the gun wasn't seen."

"All right. Fine. And just to satisfy me, suppose Blanding disregarded that and laid hands on you?"

"I'd shoot him," she replied, with a somber flash of eyes.

"You'd kill him!"

"Oh, no. I'd just blow an arm or a leg off."

"Lark!" Stanley believed she had the spirit to do as she

threatened. She was positively electrifying. "But can you shoot well enough?"

"I reckon so."

"Come out here," he rejoined, leaping up. "I'll put up my hat for you."

He stepped out from behind the rock, into more open ground, and finding a desirable snag, some twenty steps distant, he hung his sombrero upon it.

"There. I'll bet you can't hit it," he declared.

"That?" she asked with scorn. "I can hit that with my eyes shut."

"I'll not be satisfied until you show me you can shoot straight enough to protect yourself. If you can—then I'll not be so fussy about these lonely stunts of yours."

"But why waste shells? They're expensive," she returned.

"Lark, you're crawling now. I'll bet you can't hit that hat once out of five shots."

"What'll you bet?" she retorted, spurred by his ridicule.

"Anything. Give you any odds. If you're not kidding me, it's a good chance for you to earn some money."

"Oh, I couldn't bet money, worse luck. Mr. Wade gives me a weekly allowance, but I'm saving that."

"I'd hate to take your money. But I'll risk mine. What have you to bet against, say—the two hundred dollars you need so badly for your ranch?"

"Two hundred dollars! . . . Stanley, are you out of your head?"

"Certainly. It's a blissful state. . . . What can you gamble on your skill with a gun?"

"I haven't anything. You know that. You're just—what did you accuse me of—just kidding me."

"Indeed I am not," he retorted gaily. "Would you risk a kiss?"

She had been wide-eyed and eager, a little incredulous, and now she blushed.

"Don't be silly, Stanley."

"Silly! I wish you knew how far I am from silly just this moment. . . . Surely you can risk a kiss—if you're such a good shot. A kiss is a kiss, you know. No, you don't know!"

"I never kissed any man save Dad. But I'd not mind kissing you—if it wasn't for Marigold. You know she wouldn't like it. And of course you'd have to tell her."

"Do you imagine Marigold tells *me* everything?" he demanded banteringly.

"That's not the question."

"Oh, you make a distinction between Marigold, and you and me. Thank you, Lark. . . . Well, will you bet?"

"It's highway robbery, Stanley," she rejoined, smiling at him.

"That so? I see you still have my scarf. I'll include that in the bet."

"This is just a—a trick of yours to make me a present of—of money," she protested.

"No. I stand a mighty good chance of being kissed. . . . Lark, you have the reddest, sweetest lips, like ripe cherries."

His mood worked upon her, as he had divined it would. She was a primitive child of the open, and she loved him. Again there was a telltale sign of that disrupting fact.

"You don't stand one chance in a hundred," she said. "Unless this gun won't shoot straight." She turned the blue, shiny revolver in her hand.

"It's perfectly accurate."

"Very well. Say good-by to your money," she replied coolly, as she raised the gun. It was something to see the way she aimed. When she first pulled the trigger, the hammer fell upon the one empty chamber. Then she shot five times in such rapid succession that Stanley could scarcely distinguish between the explosions.

He thought he had detected a movement in the hat, but it did not fall off the snag.

"I've won, Lark," he cried, like a boy.

"You have? Go see."

Stanley ran to secure the hat. To his amazement there were two holes in the crown and three in the broad brim.

"Holy smoke! You've ruined my new sombrero," he exclaimed, running back to show it to her.

"You dared me to bet, Stanley Weston. . . . Let's see. Five, all right. I reckoned I'd missed that last shot. See this hole at the edge? I pulled off a little on that one."

"I'll say you can shoot, Lark," he declared in excited admiration. "Honest, I thought you were talking through your hat. And you made holes in *my* hat. Serves me right. . . . Lark, you can mosey around alone any time or anywhere if you'll pack that gun. I hope Blanding runs into you and gets worse than fresh, damn him!"

"I don't. He's a disagreeable person."

"Lark, where and how did you ever learn to shoot that way?"

"Jake taught me. I got so good that I could hit jack rabbits from my horse. Our farm was overrun with jacks. We had to fight them. Of late years, though, we couldn't afford to shoot them. That's another reason why the ranch ran down."

"Well, you've won the bet. I'll pay when we get back to town. And to be honest, Lark, I'm glad to lose the scarf and two hundred dollars, but darned sorry to lose what I bet for."

She slipped the gun in her pocket and stepped close to him. She paled. Her dark eyes glowed with a solemn, mournful, beautiful light. She caught her breath. Then the blood came burning back to cheek and brow.

"If it means so—so much, I'll pay the same as if I'd lost," she said.

This was Stanley's punishment. He had trifled with fire. He had intrigued innocence. And he deserved the dismay that overtook him.

"Oh, it wouldn't be fair—Lark," he stammered, trying to laugh, throbbingly aware of her nearness.

"It'd be a kind of farewell, Stanley," she replied earnestly. She wanted to kiss him. The manifestations were well-nigh irresistible.

"Wait, then, Lark, until it's time for farewell," he said lamely, and he turned away, shaking inwardly with the force of suppression.

"I didn't mean to call your bluff, as Marigold says,"

replied Lark sagely, "but I reckon you don't care so awful much about that kiss."

"Reserve judgment, please," went on Stanley lightly. "I'm not forgetting that I have your word."

He strode toward camp, down through brush and trees, in and among the stones, with Lark keeping pace with him. She could walk as well as she could ride. They did not have much to say during this tramp. Stanley was almost running away from temptation. Every minute he was aware of Lark's presence.

Stanley was right in his calculation, and came out on the slope at a point above Lark's tent. It had been his hope that Lark and he could make an unobtrusive return to camp. In vain!

"Stanley, the innocent always get caught," remarked Lark subtly, and her laugh made him thrill. After all, she was not so simple. "My cousin sees us."

"I'm glad of it," returned Stanley savagely.

12

LARK GIGGLED as she turned aside at her tent. She had a well-developed sense of humor. There was Marigold sitting bolt upright in her hammock, watching them.

"I don't know whether to say good night or good luck."

Stanley paused to give Lark the benefit of abounding admiration. "So you're a thoroughbred, too, along with a lot of other things! All right, then say good night. It's coming to me, if I don't mistake Marigold's expression."

He strode straight down and across the intervening distance to where Marigold and her noisy guests were gathered. They quieted by the time he arrived. Marigold's handsome face wore a most natural flush, very becoming, and her eyes had a devilish gleam.

"Look at that," he said, holding up his sombrero between Marigold's eyes and the light. "See the holes?"

"What are they?" asked Marigold icily.

"Bullet holes. I bet Lark she couldn't shoot. But she could, believe thou me. I lost my bet and my perfectly good sombrero."

"Is that all you lost?" asked Marigold with cool sarcasm. Her hard, bright blue eyes fastened upon him as if he seemed to be betraying something unfamiliar to her.

"Well, yes, I reckon—all the material loss I sustained," returned Stanley, just as coolly.

"Did you forget you'd promised to take us riding again this afternoon?" asked Marigold.

"Well, I sure did. I'm sorry, Marigold," he replied contritely, for he had made the promise. "But we can still go."

"It's too late. Almost dinnertime. You've been gone for hours."

Marigold was furious, and very likely more than that. Stanley replied: "So I have been. Well! . . . I went off on a long hike. On the way back I ran into Lark. I really didn't note the time."

Marigold made an eloquent gesture to her friends, sitting and lounging around. "Girls, you hear that? We've got to congratulate Lark. Any girl who can make my husband-to-be forget himself takes the prize, believe me."

"Say, don't talk about Lark in that kidding way when you mean otherwise," said Stanley sharply. "It was my fault and I'm sorry. I forgot the date. I apologize. . . . All the same, I'd like to remind you that you were dead asleep when I came out of my tent."

The girls saved the situation for Stanley by affecting not to grasp any significance in Marigold's attitude. They made merry over it until Marigold, always amenable and a good sport, fell in line with them. She never mentioned the circumstance to him again. Moreover, she was so friendly and jolly with Lark that Stanley reproached himself for imagining she was jealous. Marigold was hard to fathom. She veered with the winds. Temper was her worst fault.

That night a rider from Blanding's outfit visited camp and sang cowboy songs for Marigold and her party. Stanley had heard them many a time, but enjoyed them more than ever before because of Lark's undisguised pleasure. How unusual for a girl who had lived half her life on the range never to have heard cowboy songs! That was Lark.

Stanley went to bed while some of the others were still up, laughing round the campfire. The day had been far more exhausting than if he had toiled at manual labor. Once comfortably settled in his blankets he gave himself over to a résumé of the incidents which had led up to Lark's disturbing disclosure. He wanted to approach that gradually, so as to resist its gloriously provocative truth. But long before he got to his meeting with Lark, he fell asleep.

Stanley awoke with a start. Someone was slapping on his tent at a point near his head.

"Weston, wake up," said a low, hoarse voice.

"Hello! Yes. I'm awake," replied Stanley, raising his head.

"Better get up an' see what's goin' on round here," went on the voice, sharper and more hurried.

"What!—Who're you?" demanded Stanley.

He heard only quick, thumping footsteps, dying away. Stanley sat up, and swore under his breath. He had not recognized that voice, but he suspected the speaker had disguised it. That in itself was ominous. Moreover, the content was a warning. What could be going on around camp that would prompt someone, most likely one of the hired hands, to wake him in the dead of night, Stanley wondered.

The upshot of his cogitations was that he dressed quickly. Putting on his heavy sheepskin-lined coat, he went out. Judging by the moon the hour was past midnight. It was almost as bright as day. Stanley peered in the direction the footsteps had taken, which was toward the chuck wagon. The men had a tent over there by the corral. Jeff slept under his wagon. Had this midnight prowler been one of these men? Stanley strode across the moon-blanched space.

"Hey, who called me?" he asked loudly.

He received no answer. That nonplused him. If his visitor belonged to this camp he would most certainly be awake, and, if he refused to answer, the reason could only be that he desired to hide his identity. Stanley did not repeat his call. He went back.

The main campfire had burned down to a bed of dull red coals, which yet emitted heat. The air was piercingly cold. Stanley stooped to warm his hands, which he put over his ears. Kneeling there he gazed all around wonderingly, anxiously, beginning to resent his arousal. Nothing was going on around camp! There was no one up. The silence was profound. But it really was worth the trouble and discomfort of getting up and coming out to see the cold brilliant beauty of the country under the moon. The pines were sighing low, the ridge shining silver and black, the valley fading away into weird gloom.

All at once Stanley sustained a stinging intimation. It was hardly a thought. It must have been mental telepathy. The occurrence this night disturber had warned him about had to do with Marigold. The instant this thing was clear in Stanley's puzzled mind he repudiated it bitterly. Such instant suspicion was unworthy of him. But he could not eradicate it. This time it would not be dismissed at his will; it persisted.

He could at least very easily ascertain if Marigold were in her tent. Of course she would be. He walked over softly to see if the tent flaps were closed and tied, with the notched stick which held open an aperture for ventilation high up.

Marigold's tent had a fly attached, and this cast a shadow over the opening. He went close to peer sharply. The flaps were open wide. The stick lay on the ground. He called out in his consternation. No reply! Marigold was not in the tent.

Stanley plodded back, and, drawing a section of wood to the fire, he huddled down over the red coals. But that action was only instinctive. He no longer felt the cold. His intention was to sit there for a reasonable time, under the assumption that everything was all right. He knew it was not, but he meant to act as if it were.

Whoever had awakened him undoubtedly was aware that Marigold had not gone to bed at all, or else had come out after all the others had retired. This galled Stanley. The warning had been in his interest, and had come from someone who knew him, liked him, hated to be identified with something bound to cause him shame.

Half an hour dragged by. It was now near one o'clock. How inconceivable that there had been times, years ago, when Marigold would stand looking at the moon for almost hours, oblivious of her surroundings. She was quite capable of anything. He might be needlessly distressing himself, for she could have arisen because she was cold and gone in with one of the girls. That had happened before. Two thoughts inhibited his natural desire to go hunt for her—the first was that she would divine his distrust, and the second a fear that he might well have reason for his suspicion.

So there was nothing to do but sit there and wait. To go back to his bed in uncertainty was not to be considered. Time passed. The minutes grew long. Excitement gradually failed to keep him unaware of the cold. And he did not care to put on fresh wood to blaze up and betray his vigil.

The moon slanted away from the zenith. Orion sloped toward the west. Stanley refused to conjecture about the hour. He bent over the fading coals, chilled to the bone, miserable as he had never been before in his life. Still he kept sharp watch. Now and then faint sounds struck his straining ears.

At last he heard a step. He could not locate it. Presently there followed a swish of canvas, very low, but unmistakable. A glimmer of candlelight shone for a second in Marigold's tent, then went out. Stanley shook with more than the cold. Should he go to bed and let it pass, or speak to her? Then anger seized him. Without more ado he leaped up and strode swiftly across to Marigold's tent, and bending low to the flaps, now closed, he called: "Marigold, where have you been?"

A tingling moment of suspense held Stanley stiff. He called her name louder.

"Oh! Is that—you, Stan?" she replied, in a startled voice, unfamiliar to Stanley.

"Yes," he replied.

"You frightened me."

"I've been waiting up hours for you. . . . Where have you been?"

"You have? But I've only been out a little while." Her voice lost its unnatural note.

Stanley consulted the stars. "It is past two o'clock. I have been up since before midnight. You were not in your tent."

"Indeed? Why all this solicitous interest so suddenly?" she asked mockingly. Marigold was herself again.

"Some man slapped on my tent—woke me up," replied Stanley, speaking low. "I answered. Then he said, 'Better get up and see what's going on round here.'"

Stanley certainly caught a sibilant sound, not unlike a hiss. Then Marigold's cold voice, high-pitched now, fell upon Stanley's throbbing ears. "The cowboys had a bottle. I heard them before I went out. They kept me awake."

"Why did you get up and go out?"

"I couldn't sleep. I wanted to get out and walk. So I did."

"Moon-gazing?" asked Stanley contemptuously.

"Yes, I did look at the moon. It was lovely."

"Did you look at it alone?"

"Stanley, would you mind going to hell?"

"I've been there for two hours tonight."

"Well, serves you right. You certainly were in heaven all afternoon. . . . Don't you imagine I have cause to lie awake—to walk alone under the trees with my trouble?"

"Sure. But not on my account," replied Stanley bitterly.

"I suppose it was *my* fault, that *you* made love to Lark."

"That's not true. I didn't."

"Bah! Any fool could have seen that from her face. The girl is mad about you."

"So that got you up in the middle of the night," asserted Stanley hotly. "Marigold, I think you are a liar."

"That is very evident. . . . Thanks, Mr. Weston. I don't care a damn what you think."

"That's just as evident. . . . Marigold, I think you went out to meet Blanding."

This hot, explosive accusation seemed to burst from Stanley against his will. At least he had not admitted it to his consciousness.

"You dirty dog!" she returned in dulcet, trilling tones. If she had flung that vulgar exclamation at him in fierce wrath, in outraged honor, he might have regretted his hasty, jealous words. As it was he drew sharply erect, as if slapped in the face, and strode silently away.

Stanley went back to bed, outwardly frozen and inwardly on fire. The end had come between him and Marigold, if she really were guilty. He knew her well enough to reason that out. If she were not, she would bring about a grand upheaval, rake him unmercifully over the coals, weep like a fountain, and then make up with him. The process had become familiar, yet had always found him vulnerable. Marigold was beautiful, and in moments of stress, when something vital hung in the balance, she was not above exploitation of that beauty, in abandoned outbursts of tears, reproaches, vows, passionate caresses and kisses, in all the blandishments of love. If she tried that again she might find him impervious. But Marigold would know. She was too wise to make that mistake.

Stanley fell into restless slumber, to dream horrid, detached, unrecognizable things, and to awaken late, sorry to see the light of day again. The sun was high and the white frost sparkled like diamonds as it melted.

Marigold, for a change, was up before any of the other girls, except Lark. Presently she approached Stanley, who was standing at the campfire. She looked splendidly, regally icy. Her eyes were like blue diamonds.

"Hold out your hand," she said imperiously, without the slightest hint of a greeting.

Stanley, too dumbfounded to bid her good morning, complied with her order. And the next instant something glittered like a sunlit dewdrop upon his palm. It was the diamond engagement ring he had given Marigold.

"There! I should have given you that days ago," she said coolly. "When you offered me my freedom . . . But I was under two strong influences—one, that I really cared for you, and the other, that my father importuned me to save his failing fortunes by marrying the Weston money."

"What—what's this?" stammered Stanley, at once sustaining a pang and a leap of his heart. "My ring! . . . You mean—this is the end?"

"Yes, darling, the parting of the ways," she went on. "Last night, while you thought I was pulling some rotten stuff with Blanding, I was up pacing to and fro, trying to fight it out. You had fallen for Lark, and she, poor kid, was mad about you. And I had been indiscreet enough to allow a conceited cowboy to compromise me. It was a lovely mess. But I solved it, and when I got back to my tent I was rewarded by your insult."

"I'm sorry, Marigold. I apologize. But if you are fair, you will agree that I have had some cause to—to—"

"Yes. But you went too far, Stanley. I'm through. And you are going to ride over to see me tell Blanding where he gets off."

She was icy, superb and inscrutable. Stanley could not probe the depths of her. But it was impossible to doubt her passion. Her stormy eyes locked with his another instant and then she turned away.

Stanley stood there like a statue until Lark came hurriedly up. "Oh, what is the matter, Stanley?" she asked entreatingly. "Mari looked furious!"

For answer Stanley held out his open hand with the glittering diamond.

"Oh!" cried Lark, her eyes dilating, and she shrank. "Marigold has—broken your engagement?"

"She ditched me cold, Lark. Short and sweet," replied Stanley heavily.

"On my—account! . . . Because—because—" gasped the girl wildly.

"I don't think so. . . . Last night I was up late. Marigold had not gone to her tent. When she returned I accused her of meeting Blanding. She called me a dirty dog, and this morning returned my ring. I don't quite get it all."

"Oh!—You are not a-a-not that," cried Lark hotly. "She did meet him—if not last night—at other times. I know. Coil told me. . . . Oh, Stanley, this is dreadful."

"Yes, and we are in for more," replied Stanley tersely. "Marigold said she was taking me over to hear her tell Blanding where he gets off."

Lark stared at him in uncomprehending grief and walked away to her tent. Stanley put the ring in his pocket and sat down beside the fire with his back to the tents. Breakfast was called. When they were all seated, except Marigold, she appeared, approaching from where the cowboys were saddling the horses.

"Friends, I don't want to spoil the party," announced Marigold, "but I'm asking you all to see me through an unpleasant little job. We are riding over to call upon Mr. Blanding. . . . After that there is no reason why we can't have a wonderful time."

Her voice, like ice ringing on glass, scarcely needed the confirmation of her scornful, beautiful face to make plain to everyone that something was seriously amiss. Breakfast was not the usual merry meal, and certainly was not lingered over. Immediately afterward Marigold asked her guests and the cowboys to mount, and she led the way down to the level valley. Once there she urged her horse to a lope and headed for Blanding's camp.

The morning was clear and bright, with a frosty gold sheen upon the sage. Stanley kept with the group, who followed closely upon Marigold. The ride did not lack excitement. For Stanley there was more than that. If he did not miss his guess, Mr. Blanding was in for a few bad moments. Stanley knew what it meant to incur the wrath of Marigold Wade.

They soon arrived at the camp of the wild-horse drivers. It appeared to be a small tent settlement, but the Indians and cowboys were conspicuously absent. At Coil's halloo several men appeared, the last of whom was Blanding. Upon seeing Marigold's party line up, he started and his handsome face flamed red and then paled. But he strode out, a superb figure, booted and belted, with a gun swinging at his hip.

"What do you want, Weston?" he asked sharply, as he halted in front of the horses.

"Blanding, I'm not making this call," replied Stanley, as sharply as had the other.

"Well, then, who the hell—?" he growled.

Marigold's high voice interrupted him. "*I* am making the call, Mr. Blanding. I brought my party to hear me tell you something."

"Oh, yeah?" exclaimed Blanding resentfully. But he was amazed and nonplused.

"My purpose is to correct an impression of theirs and to set you right," went on Marigold, and her scorn was like a lash. "Mr. Blanding, I did you the honor to imagine I was in love with you. I flirted with you; I danced and rode with you. . . . Only yesterday I discovered the real reason why Stanley Weston knocked you senseless and had you dragged out of his bunkhouse. He should have horsewhipped you, because your implication was a rotten lie. . . . To my shame and disgust I confess I let you kiss me. But that was all. . . . I think you are a despicable blackguard, and I wouldn't wipe my dusty boots on you!"

Having delivered this denunciation, Marigold waited a moment to see if the livid Blanding had any reply; then she wheeled her horse and spurred him away. The others seemed unable to react quickly, held there by the spectacle of a man's malignant passion. It was as if a mask had been removed from Blanding's handsome face, to disclose something hideous. Lark was the first to recover, and she shot away like the wind. Stanley was the last to turn away his horse. Marveling at Marigold, thrilling at the audacious way in which she had seen fit to face Blanding, Stanley thoughtfully followed the others back to camp.

Excitement prevailed there, judging from the actions of the cowboys. But Stanley accosted the cook.

"Jeff, who was it that called me last night?"

"Was you called? Woke up?"

"I sure was."

"Doggone if I know. Let's ask the boys."

Stanley propounded that query in no uncertain words. The cowboys expressed surprise and denied any knowledge of it. Each one of them faced Stanley clear-eyed and frank.

"Well somebody did, and I prowled around for hours."

"Mebbe one of Blanding's riders come up," suggested Jeff. "They've gone dotty down there. Must have been up all night so's to get out before daylight. The wild-hoss drive is on."

"What? Today?"

"Sure is."

"Who told you?"

"Nobody. I got eyes for myself. Look out on the sage."

In the clear, bright sunshine Stanley could see far across the valley. Miles away, far beyond the limits of the fence, clouds of dust and moving dark lines attested to the approach of bands of wild horses.

"How come, Landy?" he asked.

"Reckon Blanding was lyin' about the start," replied Elm. "An' the hosses have moved quicker than expected."

"The Injuns must have started them yesterday," said Jeff. "This mornin' when I got up, about daylight, I seen Blanding's riders streakin' it out there. So the drive's on."

"It can't come too soon for me," declared Stanley. "But will the big bunch of horses come in today?"

"If they don't, they'll sure be hittin' it for the Oregon. Them horses are movin'."

"Looks as if they were milling," replied Stanley, shading his eyes with his hands.

"They're not bein' crowded, that's sure," returned Landy Elm. "I reckon Blanding's outfit is stretched out beyond the end of the fence. They'll hold what hosses are movin' from passin' on. Then when the Indians come down behind the big bunch Blanding will close in."

"The drive is on!" shouted Stanley. He felt relieved at the prospect of action and excitement. "Lark! Lark! Are you going to miss it?"

"Miss what? Stanley, your voice has a funny sound," responded Lark, emerging from her tent.

"Has it? No wonder. Lark, the wild-horse drive has started."

"What!" she cried wildly.

"Sure. Look at the dust and black strings out there on the sage. Call the others."

Then he repaired to the campfire site and vigorously gave the log he had sat upon last night a shove and a kick onto the still smoldering coals. He was neither sentimental nor moody any longer. There seemed to be high-pressure voltage somewhere in his interior.

When he got the fire to blaze up he went back to his tent for his field glasses. With these he hurried to the rock across the stream and, climbing upon it, took a look at the hazy, spotted horizon.

As if by magic the sage flat had become a scene of extraordinary color and action. Over the gray sage floated low clouds of dust. From out of these clouds shot black objects: wild horses, manes and tails flying. It was too far to estimate numbers, but there were many animals. One bunch would appear out of a mantle of dust only to disappear into another. Stanley wished to ascertain if the horses were approaching in his direction. But of this he could not be sure. There was incessant movement across a wide front.

"Oh, let me look!" cried an eager voice. Lark came running. She was bareheaded. Her waving hair shone in the sun. Cheeks and lips flashed red. She looked like a lithe, round-limbed boy in her jeans and jacket. She scurried up the rock with the agility of a squirrel.

"Well, Lark," he said, handing her his glass. "By noon this valley will be black with wild horses."

"I see—I see," she cried, before she took the glasses. After a long survey through them she said: "Scared! Not stampeded yet . . . Riders out to the left. Oh, the devils! It'll be like running horses over a precipice. Stanley, can't we do something?" she asked appealingly. "Just you and me! The rest of this outfit wouldn't move a finger."

"Right," laughed Stanley. "I'm afraid you and I are almost as bad, as far as doing anything is concerned. It's a free range. The horses are wild all right, but they are on the Indian reservation and really belong to the Indians. Blanding pays them a dollar a head. It's a business transaction. The ranchers, I daresay, except Dad and I, are keen on ridding the range of wild horses. So what can we do?"

"I see. *You* couldn't do anything if that's all you care," she retorted.

"Care! See here, Lark, I don't like your tone. I do care. But it's ridiculous even to think of stopping Blanding."

"You could buy those riders off. You're rich. You don't care a lot for money, judging from the way you gamble."

"Lark, you're a little unreasonable," returned Stanley, nettled despite his understanding of her. "If I did buy those riders off now, they'd pull the drive later."

"You don't love wild horses."

"Yes I do."

"Then you could shoot Blanding," said the girl, without heat or any semblance of agitation. Her hands were steady on the leveled glasses.

"Me? Not much!"

"You could pick a fight with him. Blanding packs a gun. But he wouldn't know what to do with it, facing a real man. You could make him draw—and shoot him. Oh, I don't mean kill him, unless in self-defense. But you could just shoot his leg off or something."

"Gee, Lark, but you have a gentle disposition," he ejaculated, in surprise and mirth.

"If I were a man I'd do it," she snapped.

"Lark, I admire your spirit," replied Stanley seriously. "But this can lead to much trouble. You must reconcile yourself to that. Wild horses are no good. They eat the grass and drink the water that should be utilized by our stock. Their day is about done, Lark."

"Oh, you think I'm a little fool, I know," she exclaimed. "But I'm not. Wild horses have a right to their lives, at least on wild ranges like this. Stanley, if you knew anything about ranching you'd see that there's no grass out here. These horses are browsers. They live on sage and brush. They do no harm."

"Well, I like that, Lark Burrell," rejoined Stanley, offended. "If I knew anything about ranching!"

"I'd call you a tenderfoot."

"Indeed. Thanks. You must have been lying to me yesterday."

"It's a pity I wasn't," she declared.

"I'll make you beg mercy for calling me a tenderfoot!"

"I—I wouldn't have, but for this sight out here," she faltered, lowering the glasses. "I'm furious, Stanley. I was sick last night. But I'm mad now. I want to tear things."

"Please don't blame me, Lark," he said ruefully.

"Oh, if you just cared enough for me to stop them!"

"I couldn't stop them no matter how much I cared," protested Stanley, out of patience with this strange creature.

"That's not so!" cried Lark scornfully, and slipping off the stone she ran toward the fire.

Stanley picked up his discarded glasses. Her scorn touched a tender spot. Not from Lark, of all women, could he stand scorn. And with that there began forming in his consciousness the nucleus of a desire to render Blanding's labors futile.

Following Lark back to the fire, Stanley found Marigold there, looking unusually handsome with her great hollow eyes and her white face on which the red lips stood out in startling contrast. Her golden hair burned in the bright light. Stanley, reluctantly admiring her beauty, her grace, said to himself that she was something hard for a man to lose.

"Let's get started," suggested Stanley to the crowd.

"What's the hurry?" demurred Marigold.

"We might miss something," replied Evelyn.

"You'll miss your lunch, if you rush off. We'll want to stay out all day, and Jeff is fixing it up for us to take."

Stanley accosted Marigold as she stepped into her tent,

holding up the flap, The warm sunlight filtered through the canvas down upon her golden head.

"Marigold, in your heart you know I'm not to blame for this," he said.

"Men are never to blame," she returned mockingly. "Have you any more to say?"

"No. I accept my dismissal," he answered huskily.

She gave him a passionate, blue-flashing gaze. "I wonder. . . . All right, Stan. Give the ring to Lark."

Stanley wheeled away, his hand clenched tightly. Marigold could keep her secrets, but she had pierced his. The low, flute-like, taunting laugh lingered in his ears.

A little later, on his way to the horses, he encountered Lark, leading her horse out. She transfixed him with dark, tragic eyes.

"Oh, Stanley, she never spoke to me!—She never looked at me!"

13

THE COWBOYS led the saddled horses out for the girls to mount. Marigold as usual was the last. While they called gaily for her to hurry up she calmly stood before her tent door looking across the camp. Lark sat her mustang out on the rise of ground watching the valley. Stanley gazed from Marigold across to Lark, and all of a sudden something hard and bitter was wrenched out of his soul. He was free. Marigold had delivered him from what would have become hateful bondage. Her reasons had undoubtedly been generous, aside from her own motives.

Landy Elm stood high in his stirrups, pointing with a long arm out to the sage.

"The wild hosses are comin'."

Stanley leaped into his saddle. "All set. Let's go," he yelled.

Lark was off like a flash. The rest of the riders bunched and rode down off the ridge toward the flat.

"Landy, keep an eye on that girl," ordered Stanley, pointing to Lark.

"Okay, boss. I will if I can keep her in sight," replied Elm, spurring ahead.

"Straight across and climb out. We'll follow," yelled Stanley.

Far out on the sage there was a black and yellow bulge on the horizon. It resembled the smoke of a brush fire, creeping low. When Stanley got down to the level floor of the valley, all he could see was murky clouds.

Lark did not head straight across, in the direction Stanley had elected to go. She made for the point of the opposite ridge, far to the left. Landy was running his horse, but not closing the space between him and Lark.

"Let's go!" screamed Marigold.

"Look out for holes!" admonished Stanley, and spurred his black.

They were off in a bunch. Stanley had no wish to race, and the cowboys did not extend themselves. The girls with the other boys had a merry go of it. Marigold forged ahead. On her white horse, and wearing her red coat, she made a beautiful, colorful picture against the sage. Stanley muttered another grim farewell to his old sweetheart.

It was three or four miles across that flat to the opposite ridge. Marigold and her friends made it in short order, with Stanley and the cowboys bringing up the rear. Lark and Landy Elm showed darkly silhouetted against the sky from the ridge top. They had halted and were watching. The slope was gradual, an easy climb for a horse. Stanley ran his gaze along the face of the ridge, observing that it gradually grew steeper, rougher, higher, until it formed a wall which no horse could surmount.

"Pretty foxy stunt, I'll say," a cowboy remarked.

"What is?" asked Stanley, interested. They had brought the horses to a walk at the base of the slope.

"This drive. Place was made for a trap. Us fellows ought to be kicked for lettin' a dumb cowboy who ain't no cowboy at all pull this stunt."

"Righto," agreed Coil Bruce. "It's been gallin' me."

"The Indians put Blanding on, fellows," said Stanley. "Don't forget that."

"Are you going to let Blanding drive Sage Hill Range?" asked Coil curiously.

"There's no law to prevent him, but I'll have a go at it."

They ascended to the ridge top, from which a wonderful view unfolded itself. This point was fully a hundred feet above the sage, like a promontory running out into the sea. It, and in fact the whole long ridge, had hidden from the sightseers a wide, deep bay which cut into the mountain side, but different from the trap indentation in that it had not abrupt walls. All across this gray expanse, and far out on the sage to the left, five or six miles distant, rolled a long, broken line of moving dust clouds and black patches.

"Boss, they're sure on the run," called Landy, as Stanley rode up.

"So I see. Some sight. What'll we do, Landy? We may be stuck here, if we wait too long. . . . I told Lark to ride straight across, so that we'd not have far to go to the trap. That's our objective, if we're going to see the best of this drive."

"I took in the lay of the land," rejoined Lark. "We can ride the ridge or go low down along the bank."

"Very good. Then it resolves to how long we'll stay here. What do you say, Landy?"

"I reckon we needn't hurry," replied that worthy, scanning the sage. "All these wild horses are runnin' east. An' they'll keep straight on till they're swung from the far side, by that bunch of riders. They'll crowd the horses in an' then the fence will turn them up the valley."

"Marigold, what do you think?" asked Stanley.

"Heavens! Listen to Stan, girls," retorted Marigold. "He concedes me capacity for thought."

"Say, can't any of you express an opinion?"

"It's a wonderful sight, Stanley."

"I'll say it is."

Landy approached Stanley. "Boss, you remember, the

other day Blanding's outfit didn't have any gate to their trap."

"That's so. But they had time to build one yesterday."

"It'll be a circus if they didn't."

Stanley dismounted and moved out on the rocks. While doing so he caught a glimpse of Lark's face. That abruptly changed the tenor of his thought. She was a child of nature, a little mystic in some sense, and passionately fond of horses, in fact of all animals. This drive would be an ordeal for her. And if the drive made her wretched, what would the mess in that trap tomorrow do to her? For that matter Stanley imagined it would make all the girls sick. Straightway he became thoughtful again. To hell with this handsome Blanding anyhow!

With that change in his feelings he attended to the scene out in front. The broken line of horses must have been six or eight miles long, as far as he could see. Perhaps it extended out far beyond the limit of sight. There were probably thousands of horses. The Indians had been working them down on that side of the mountain for days.

As Stanley watched, slowly the whole pall approached and enlarged, until he could ascertain that the movement had not yet become swift, though it was evident to him, as Lark had said, that the wild horses were scared. He sat there on the rock for fully half an hour, aware of the others behind, but with his attention mainly on the drive.

Bands of horses rolled out of dust clouds, only to be swallowed up by others.

"Hear that?" Lark cried out sharply. "Guns! They've begun to shoot. Now they'll crowd the horses in."

"Boss, Miss Lark has called the turn," shouted Elm. "The big drive is on."

Stanley listened until he could hear the faint report of firearms. On that still morning, gunshots could be distinguished for several miles. He stood up.

"It won't be long now," yelled a cowboy.

Indeed the scene was transforming. The inside end of the hazy pall thinned out near the curve of slope a mile to Stanley's right. Scattered small bunches of horses appeared there. Following the line with his vision, he saw the swell of the dust cloud, massed in the center. While he gazed, the gap between the moving line and the end of the trap fence narrowed and closed. The wild horses were inside.

It became fascinating, then, for Stanley to watch the oncoming of that wild, dust-shrouded army. In spots a black bobbing line of horses kept ahead of the smother. Gunshots sounded less faint and far away. To the right, straggling horses trooped in toward the hill, halted to look, ran on again, wheeled and fled back. These would escape the drive, for it appeared that the riders were now working away from each end toward the middle. The long ridge upon which the watchers stood and the outburst fence would take care of the wings of this flying mass. A brisk wind had sprung up, blowing from the horses toward them. That was what had lifted the mushrooming dust clouds on high. The boom of guns grew more distinct for a few moments, and then strangely began to die away in another sound—a low, continuous roar.

"Hey, boss, we'd better be goin'," called Landy. "Miss Lark is beatin' it back along the slope."

"Come on," shrilled Marigold.

Ironshod hoofs cracked the rocks behind Stanley. The horses moved off, and gay shouts fell upon Stanley's ears. Still he lingered. Soon the dust storm, wedge-shaped, swept across the valley at a point opposite his position. From this wedge, in toward him, the line was no line at all, but a broken scattering of blotches of color and shrouds of dust, some of them lifting, others on the move. The roar of hoofs grew plain, but as the main mass of horses was two miles from him, and speeding on toward the fence, he expected the sound to diminish, which in short order it did.

Stanley returned to mount. His companions were already out of sight on the brush ridge. He took one more look from that viewpoint, thrilling at the color, the action, the diminishing roar, and yet somehow cold to the project. Horseflesh for chicken feed! Did he need to be influenced by Lark Burrell to feel disgust at that? Not honest work, not real sport, but greed! He felt that he was growing moody.

Whereupon he headed Blackie up the ridge, following the tracks of the horses ahead. If Lark had led the advance, as no doubt she had, the trail she left spoke volumes for her range riding. For a time Stanley had to attend to loose slides of rock, treacherous places, thickets of brush, downed timber and great splintered sections of cliff, so that he could not keep track of the wild-horse drive. At length he got out of the roughest going, to surmount a bulge of slope, from which he saw the others strung out ahead and below. Far to the fore Lark's cream-colored pony shone in the sunlight. She was halfway to the head of the trap.

Stanley took a glance over the sage behind him and to the right. Above the point which he had just vacated, a plain-wide, hovering dust cloud moved across and in toward the fence opposite. The obstruction would turn the wild horses, sooner or later, and then the drive would be straight up the valley, wedging sharply toward the apex and the trap.

"I hope he breaks his neck," muttered Stanley, and rode on. In due time he caught up with Doris and Evelyn, who were fighting the brush.

"Hang close to me, girls," called Stanley, riding around them. "I'll crash the trail for you."

He led them a pretty hard race at that, but made it easier, and eventually they came out on the lower bank, where traveling was still rough but level. Stanley could see only the inside section of the fence, perhaps a mile or more of it, for the outside had been swallowed up by dust. Soon Stanley and his followers reached ground upon which they could gallop, except over the heads of gullies, and in quick time reached the constricted neck of the valley and the wall above it. Marigold and her contingent sat on their horses here, waiting. But Lark and Landy Elm had dismounted to tie their mounts, and to go on foot clear to the point above the gate of the trap.

"When is lunchtime?" asked someone.

"Any time," replied Stanley. "Landy has left the lunches and canteens here."

"Carry on, girls. Let's not let my cousin show us up," said Marigold. "I tore my pants back there, and now I don't care what happens."

"Tie up down here by Landy's horse," called Stanley, looking around. "It's back from the rim and the horses won't get scared."

On foot, presently, he was free to stride along the wall toward where it converged to the narrow gateway. And again the nature of that horse trap struck him forcibly. From this side the thing looked even more deadly than from the other, or from below on the flat. Not until he joined Lark and Landy, though, did he see the gate. It lay on the ground right under the point, and consisted merely of light posts strung close together on wire. A dozen men could run with that gate and close it quickly.

Lark sat out on the extreme edge, gazing down the valley. She appeared to be hunched over, in a stiff, if not unnatural, pose. A corner of the bright scarf she had won from Stanley fluttered in the breeze.

Upon Stanley's approach, Landy, who was standing, turned to him.

"Boss, she's cryin'," he whispered. "I thought she looked funny, but I wasn't sure till I got here."

"Landy, she loves wild horses and this drive made her sick."

"I reckoned it was that. But, boss, if she feels so bad now, what'll she do when this hole gets full of screamin', snortin', kickin' hosses, breakin' their legs on the rocks, tearin' their guts out on the snags?"

"I don't know, Landy. If it gets as bad as that I'll be sick, too."

"If these girls don't all get upset, I'll be surprised."

"Hasn't fazed them yet," replied Stanley, who had glanced backward to see the others eating lunch.

"Lark, they're eating lunch," he called. "Will you have some?"

"I couldn't eat," she answered mournfully.

She kept her face averted and a steady gaze down the

valley. Stanley thought it would be a kindness to let her alone. Besides, the dark mood that had been only intermittent now shut down upon him persistently.

"Landy, fetch me a sandwich and a drink of water," said Stanley, finding himself a seat. Upon Landy's return he asked: "What do you make of that dusty melee down there?"

"Millin', I reckon," observed the cowboy. "Anyway, they've slowed up for the finish. Sooner or later there'll be a hell-roarin' stampede up this chute."

"I hope it's late."

"Why so, boss?"

"Well, if Blanding had those horses trapped now he'd begin that tailing stunt—which I don't want to see."

"Reckon they'll begin that as soon as it's light enough to see in the mornin'."

"Blanding hasn't trapped these horses yet," added Stanley ponderingly.

Landy gave him a thoughtful glance and wended his way back to the others. Whereupon Stanley ate his sandwich, drained the cup, all the while thoughtful on his own behalf. He leaned back against the slant of rock where he had chosen to sit and closing his eyes tried to puzzle out what obsessed him. There was a disturbance, but it was not caused by Marigold's swift, relentless renunciation of their relationship. Nor was Lark responsible, he was sure. Something was twisting in his mind. It had to do with Blanding—with the dislike Stanley felt had grown since last night, an intuitive, unfathomable something—with the capture of these wild horses—with the vague idea, born of hope, that Blanding might slip up on his precious deal of horseflesh for chicken feed. Stanley got so far, then his consciousness clamped on that idea of a slip-up. The horses were not caught yet. Even if they were imprisoned they might escape—might be helped to freedom. There!

"Stanley, please come here," called Lark, disrupting his train of thought just when it had struck fire.

He hastened over the rocks to her position. Lark was not crying now, though traces of tears were visible. She looked shaken, spent.

"What is it, Lark?"

"I don't want anybody near me, but I—I better have."

"Why, child—"

"I'm no child—but a ter-rible woman."

"Yes, you're very terrible," he said, trying to laugh.

"Stanley, this wild-horse drive was bad enough to make me go all to pieces," she went on, very low, and she turned to see if anyone else was near. "But for Marigold to—to cut me as she has! . . . She looked at me once—down there on the point. Such eyes she has! I nearly dropped off my horse. . . . Oh, she hates me!"

"Hardly that, Lark," returned Stanley kindly. "She's in a temper, and you're all upset."

"Upset! My heart is broken. I feel like jumping off this cliff. Please stay by me, Stanley. . . . It's hard waiting. If the horses would only come! Then I'll get furious—I'll want to kill that Blanding."

"I'll stay, Lark," he replied softly, and he yearned to go on and tell her that presently, when he got over his own rage and pain, when a decent interval had lapsed, he meant to ask her if he could not stay by her always.

Moments sped by. The picnic party behind were making merry; the wind freshened, coming laden with a mixed odor of dust, sage and horses; far down the wide end of the triangle a whirling, yellowish mantle, valley wide, appeared to have halted, like the lodging of a cloud against a mountain top. Stanley had lost the train of thought which sent heat along his veins. His gaze passed from Lark's bonny bent head, always to come back again. He must plan so that she would never believe she had come between him and Marigold. He could blame himself.

After a while Stanley became aware that the cowboys were behind him, speculating on the drive.

"Won't be long now," remarked Landy.

"Nope. They've straightened out again."

"I'm lookin' for a stampede when the bunch packs in his bottleneck."

"Like as not. I hope they stampede before they get down into this narrow part."

Stanley saw a long, bobbing, speckled drove of wild

horses coming like the wind. The dust lifted behind them. On each flank the line thinned out, with stragglers racing apart. Again the report of guns grew audible.

Lark nervously got up and stepped back from the precipitous wall. At that point the distance down to the level appeared to be scarcely forty feet. Maddened wild horses might attempt to scale it. Stanley changed his position and stood some few yards from Lark. Then the other girls came trooping down, excited, curious.

"Look! Must be all the wild mustangs in the West!" exclaimed Doris, who was hanging on to Marigold.

The wild horses came on apace, raising less dust as they swept up the valley, due to the richer covering of grass and sage. A low rumble smote Stanley's ear. He conjectured that there was a tremendous herd. The possible brutality of the drive struck him mute, when all the others, except Lark, were giving vent to their feelings.

On they came! The left flank sheered into the stream, and great flashing splashes of water moved forward, shining in the sun. In the center of the line a V-shaped, solid mass was approaching at breakneck speed. The leader was a white horse, easily discernible as a stallion because of his crested neck. His followers spread wedge-shaped back into the dust. To the right a flank of lean mustangs came sweeping around like a wheel. The paces closed up with dark horses stretched low, running wild; and now the narrowing valley had an unbroken front clear across. The rumble became a roar.

"Boss, I reckon it ain't too safe here for the girls," yelled Landy.

"Take them back higher," returned Stanley, agreeing with him. Then he called Lark.

If she heard she gave no sign. Her face was white, her eyes shot level lightning at the onrushing herd. Stanley remained with her, sharing her risk, if not the intensity of her emotions.

Yet the spectacle was grand. It might be a shambles in a few moments, but just now the sweeping flood of variegated color, under a mantle of yellow dust, was tremendously stirring. Stanley suddenly sustained a poignant re-

gret. Why had he not destroyed the fence on the far side
of that trap? With his horse he could have opened up a
wide break. But neither his regret nor his curse stayed the
flight.

Half a mile yet! The roar swelled loud enough to
drown the gunshots. The pall of dust rose above the wes-
tering sun, which shone a dull magenta hue through the
yellow curtain. The daylight perceptibly darkened.

No one could tell how deep that mob of horses might
be. The front line showed a few hundred. But it might be
a mile deep—two miles, in which case the havoc would
be all the more terrible. Far better for these wild crea-
tures to have been heading for a precipice! That would be
merciful compared with this fate.

The swelling roar rolled into thunder. Individual horses
now stood out clearly, with the lean white stallion still
leading, and tearing behind him, all across the suddenly
constricting neck of the valley, blacks and bays, reds and
blues, iron-grays and creams, sweeping on, sweeping on
in unified action, wild, ragged, shaggy, flying.

Fifty yards from the gateway the white leader leaped
straight up to swerve aside, in supreme terror of the trap.
Those horses close at his heels did likewise. They scattered before the onrushing flood. Then the stallion, without slackening his speed, raced to the left. But the flank
on that side closed before he had made a dozen jumps.
His lean nose went up. Stanley faintly caught the wild
whistle which pierced the thunder of hoofs.

The stallion leaped for the rocks, made a magnificent
bound, caught himself, shot up again, held on a precari-
ous footing, leaped the third time, to reach short and fall
sheer. He broke his back and lay with all four hoofs beating the air. One of the cowboys shot him.

His close followers dashed to and fro, only to be run
down or crowded on toward the fatal trap. In another
moment the tide of horseflesh, solid and swift, forced on
by the momentum of those behind, squeezed through the
gateway. The foremost horses freed themselves and sped
on.

Stanley did not watch them. His fascinated gaze fixed

upon the opening which was scarcely wide enough across for thirty horses to run abreast. Then the expected thing came to pass. They jammed in the gate, and from the front of this struggling, straining mass single horses, and two and threes filtered through or were propelled as if from a catapult. Some fell in their tracks; some plunged on with broken legs; some gathered speed again.

The rolling thunder underwent a change. It gradually ceased that rhythmic volume to disintegrate into a thinner, less consistent sound, still made up of pounding hoofs. But the roll and thunder were gone. A hideous screaming, crackling, wrestling clamor, above which could be heard the yells of men, dinned into Stanley's ears.

Then the dust cloud blew forward over the point, obscuring the gateway. It was thick, yellow, bringing a strangling odor of dust, sage, horses and something raw and hot. Stanley groped for Lark, and, finding her, put an arm through hers and drew her aside, farther up, where the air was clearer. She grew heavy on his arm. But he did not look at her, or have anything to say. A sense of guilt oppressed him, strong as the disgust and horror this scene had stirred.

The mantle of dust hid only that infernal gate, where pandemonium had broken loose. The upper half of the triangular enclosure lay clear to the gaze, and already hundreds of wild horses were trapped therein. Many had run to the far corner, where the stream broke down through the wall. But others, all around, were frantically attempting escape.

Stanley felt Lark's hand like a steel band on his arm. Yet she was strangely silent. He took a fleeting glance at her, unable to resist. She had been given over entirely to the shocking cruelty which she had foreseen.

Every moment added to the number of trapped horses. For the most part they appeared to be small, scraggy, scrawny, broom-tailed mustangs, certainly not worth capturing for saddle horses. But here and there ran well-conditioned animals, and now and then one that Stanley thought good enough for any man. The crippled ones augmented his wrath. They were many: some only lamed, others with broken legs, still others badly maimed.

They clogged the break in the wall, where the water poured down in a white cascade. Others pounded upon those down in the water. As the din at the gate diminshed, the shrill whistling shrieks of horses farther up in the trap grew louder. The trampling clatter weakened. Horses ran straight at the south wall and endeavored to climb it. Most of these fell and slid down, undoubtedly sustaining bad bruises and lacerations; a few in their mad longing for freedom assailed the height and gained it, to plunge away free.

But it was the brush fence that got the brunt of the attack. So many horses lunged at this that Stanely could not keep track of them. One blue roan took a flying leap and crashed over, to flounder and tear until he got rid of the confining branches. He ran up the slope and away. Another lean, long mustang, a buckskin, ugly and scrawny, but magnificent in his spirit, completely cleared the barrier. It could be done, to Stanley's intense delight. But only a great leaper, who had the intelligence to start with a long run, could make that prodigious jump. Most of the animals there came to grief. The fence had been built of trees dragged close together, with the interstices filled by brush, cactus, stumps. Here and there dead treetops, with naked snags, stood up menacingly. When a horse hit these it was bad for him.

"Oh, my God, look there!" screamed Lark suddenly, close to Stanley's ear. She pointed with a shaking hand to her right, farther down from where Stanley had been watching the fence.

He saw a gray horse, long mane and tail flying, high up on that fence, but stationary, it seemed. Stanley stared. The animal crashed over on its side, exposing a great, gory hole where a snag had entered its belly. An awful convulsive effort only gored the poor creature deeper. Stanley saw this horse disembowel itself, to sink shudderingly down, impaled on that snag.

"Let's get away from here," Stanley cried to Lark.

"No. I'll stick it out."

The din had toned down. Dust hovered over the trap, but the thick canopy had lifted. A trampling mass of horses piled through the aperture, now hazily visible. Men were shouting down there.

Stanley's eyes swept the enclosure in an attempt to estimate the catch: more than three thousand head, he felt sure. It was a sudden, stunning victory for Hurd Blanding.

He then became aware that the cowboys of Marigold's party were behind him, and the girls were approaching, all except Evelyn, who evidently felt close enough. Even at a distance she looked white and sick. Marigold's face was flushed, her eyes brilliantly large.

"Lark, you'd better stay here," suggested Stanley. "It's all over. A huge success for Blanding."

Stanley followed the cowboys down to the point. A crowd of mounted Indians on wet, dust-caked mounts filled the narrow head of the valley. They were jabbering among themselves. Near the gate a dozen or more white riders stood peering in at their captives. Several others were mounted, one of whom was Blanding, at the moment in the act of wiping a begrimed face. While he performed this task with care, his gaze was fastened upon the uninvited group up on the point. Presently he waved a scarf. This was an affront to Stanley, or so he took it, but Stanley was beyond reason. He yelled to still the rabble below. Then:

"Hey, Blanding, will you shoot these crippled and gored horses?" he called piercingly, as he pointed behind to the trap.

Blanding looked up and the thrust of his head spoke volumes.

"That's our business," he shouted.

"Well, it's a pretty dirty business," retorted Stanley.

"Hell you say!"

"Yes, the hell I say."

"It's none of yours."

"I'll make it mine. If you don't shoot these crippled horses, I will."

Here Ellery Wade appeared to remonstrate with Blanding, who cursed him roundly.

"Stan, we mean to kill all the cripples," yelled Ellery.

"Go to it, then."

Blanding ordered his men out through the gate, evidently to execute the order Stanley had demanded. Then Blanding rode over to the base of the wall, probably to make himself heard better. Stanley stepped to the edge; with that they were not far apart. He heard the others of his party crowding in behind him.

"Say, Weston, maybe you don't know you weren't invited out to see this drive," flung Blanding sarcastically.

"I didn't think I was," snapped Stanley.

"You bet you weren't. When I invited Marigold I didn't include you. Do you get that?"

"Yes, I get that."

"Then you keep your lip out of my affairs. These horses belong to me."

"Blanding, no one disputes that. I had no intention of butting in. But it's a bloody mess. If you have any decent feeling, you'll put these miserable beasts out of their agony in a hurry."

Lark had sidled closer and closer to Stanley, coming from behind.

"Can't you see the man is bad? He'd as lief shoot *you* as the horses," she whispered fiercely.

Stanley turned away from the upturned face below. A desperate note rang in Lark's voice. She was the unknown, uncertain factor here.

"Hello, Idaho, how'd you like my drive?" called Blanding tauntingly.

Lark gazed down, with no other reply than that. It was enough, Stanley thought, to confirm his own conviction about this girl. She was dangerous.

"Marigold told me about the big herd of wild horses down on the Salmon River," Blanding went on. "I'm sure going to make a drive there."

Marigold stepped forward, color flaming her cheek.

"Cut it out! This end of your damn old drive is diabolical," she flashed.

"Why, Marigold, you're getting sassy," he drawled. "You didn't talk that way a week ago."

Marigold wheeled with a passionate gesture. "Girls, he's a devil. . . . Let's get away from here."

Fortunately, gunshots distracted Stanley's attention at this point. The riders had begun to shoot the maimed horses.

"Be careful in there," yelled Blanding. "Don't crowd the bunch."

There was indeed danger of another stampede. The three riders kept away from the far end of the trap, shooting the crippled horses near at hand. Stanley noticed one wretched beast staggering along with entrails dragging on the ground. It was a pretty, long-maned mare, about ready to foal. Glad indeed was he when a bullet sent her to her knees, and another ended her existence. Stanley waited only long enough to see that Lark had already mounted Chaps, and was riding on toward the upper end of the trap. The others were taking to the saddles. He followed suit.

As they rode around the enclosure Stanley gazed down. The shooting had forced the wild horses to the extreme end of the trap, where they huddled in a dense formation, all faces turned to the riders. Stanley was the last to cross the stream above and head along the opposite slope. He gave deep scrutiny to the fatal brush fence, and his mind clamped on a daring resolve. It excluded all else, and even though he saw Lark riding far ahead he did not think of her. Far down on the valley floor he saw the Indians and riders making for their camp. But he did not think of them, while his pulse leaped.

It was dark when Stanley arrived in camp. While he unsaddled Blackie the call to supper sounded. There was no merry response. Marigold's party were worn out with travel and excitement. Marigold herself was pale and silent. Stanley deliberately tried to catch her eye, but failed.

After supper he did not approach the campfire and observed that Lark did not either. Stanley went to his tent and without taking off his clothes he lay down. His mind had been made up. He intended to slip out late in the night and let the wild horses out of the trap. If he could not open the gate he could make a hole in the fence. This idea had had its inception solely because of Lark's grief. But once the resolve was formed, he began to react to it on his own behalf. He did not intend to go to sleep.

While he lay there thinking, the girls and boys outside talked and laughed round the campfire. The shadows flickered on Stanley's tent. By and by he grew cold and drew blankets up over him. Marigold and her guests stayed up long, drinking coffee and talking. Before they went to bed Stanley fell asleep.

Sometime in the night he awakened, probably from the cold. All was still. The crowd had turned in. Looking at his watch, he was amazed to find the hour long after one o'clock. He got up and went out cautiously.

The moon was rising. The stars were bright. Like an Indian he stole off noiselessly, crossed the brook and took to the slope, working along over the trail made by the horses on their two trips toward the trap. That afternoon he had been careful to make note of how to get down there. It would be a long walk, but he preferred to make this trip on foot. Wherefore he held himself in to avoid haste, with eyes and ears vigilant.

At first he felt the cold, but after he had been traveling for a little while he warmed up. The moon sank, letting the stars shine brighter. The zest of this adventure reminded him of old boyish pranks, and something of the thrill and fight of his earlier days returned to him. What would Lark say? She would be overcome. She would pay him more than the one kiss she owed.

Coyotes yapped down in the valley; at intervals his ear registered some sound, but when he halted to listen it ceased; the wind blew in his face and he imagined he smelled smoke. Where could that come from? Perhaps Blanding had left some Indians behind to guard the trap and they had built a fire. He could ascertain presently when he got beyond the bulge of the slope. If he sighted a fire he would go far around it and high up, then descend back of the trap and make a break in the brush fence. No fear about the sharp-eyed, wild horses not finding it!

Suddenly another sound stopped him short. Like a

wind in the trees or a rushing river, far away! But there was no wind and no river. He listened. From ahead of him came a sudden roar, intermittent, then growing stronger. The horses must be moving. He ran swiftly along the trail and got around the big bench of the ridge. Here he checked his stride to a walk, until at length, emerging on the slope almost above the trap, he halted.

Dimly he could make out the floor of the valley. It was gray where the sage grew, black along the walls and ravines. The sound struck him instantly as a sliding of soft earth and gravel, a cracking and swishing of brush. Then followed the unmistakable, trampling roar of hundreds of hoofs. The wild horses were on the move. Stanley ran fast, farther along, farther down.

When he stopped again he was not far from the trap. Still the roar appeared to move away from him. As there was no wind, this could not be the case if the animals were running around the enclosure.

Suddenly he realized that the wild horses were moving uphill. His heart leaped. They had broken out. Trembling with excitement, he jumped upon a boulder. In the starlight he made out a black stream ascending the slope. It was not close, but he could discern the dark, moving belt against the gray. Cracks of hard hoofs on stone made him all the more certain. He wanted to whoop like an Indian. The sliding, rustling roar went on, swelled and then gradually lessened in volume, until it became faint and died away. The black shadow across the gray had slipped over the ridge.

"What do you know about that?" whispered Stanley to himself, sitting down in his astonishment. "They've got out! . . . They're gone!"

At that instant a light appeared below in the black shade at the foot of the slope. Stanley beheld it with startled eyes. It enlarged into a blaze. He caught sight of brush. Suddenly a flare shot up. Dead pine-needle foliage, burning like rockets! By the bright light he made out the long, dark fence. Somebody had fired it! Transfixed, Stanley watched. Who could have done that? Only one person—Lark! The flames crackled fiercely; the circle of

light widened. Stanley discerned a wide break in the fence
where the horses had escaped. He saw also that the trap,
as far around as he could view, was empty, except for a
black spot here and there, which was probably a dead
horse.

In a few moments the fire had gained such headway
that the whole enclosure was visible. The closed gate, the
steep walls, the cascade in the shadow were lighted up.

"By heck! She's done it!" he exulted under his breath.
"Nerve! Well, I guess."

Then his quick ear caught hoofbeats. He slipped off the
rock. Lark, or whoever it was, was riding up the trail. The
flare spread up the hill. Stanley soon made out a horse
with a rider. He crouched behind the rock. It might not
be Lark. Then he recognized the mustang. It was Chaps,
looking buff in the firelight. That slight, dark form astride
him could be none other than Lark. Stanley stepped out
into the trail and hailed her.

14

THE TIGHT, hot oppression in Lark's breast had loosened when the last shots of Blanding's riders assured her
that all the maimed wild horses had been put out of their
misery.

She rode away from the point without looking to see if
the rest of Marigold's party was following. As sunset was
not a great while off they would not linger much longer.
But she rode along the left wall of the trap, and, crossing
the stream, she turned Chaps on the slope and passed
close above the brush fence. There was a large boulder
marking the middle of this fence, where the butts of several brushy trees showed on the outside. With a rope on
the pommel of her saddle she could snake those trees out
of there in short order. That would make an aperture

forty feet wide. Large enough if she had no more time! But she wanted the horses to escape before she set fire to the rest of the fence.

Turning up the trail which the horses had made on the first day, Lark bent experienced eyes on the lay of the land, the rocks and trees, so that she could find her way to and fro in the dark.

On the ridge top, which she soon attained, she marked the point where the trail started down, and then had no more concern about that. She did not glance back once.

Blanding's Indians were riding weary horses across the flat below toward their camp. Blanding, with his white riders, brought up the rear. They had not left anyone on guard. Probably he had no fear that the wild horses might break out of that secure trap. It did not make any difference to Lark, however, whether he sent guards or not. After long days of strenuous toil such as his men had undergone, they would sleep. And in any event, if she thought best not to make a break in the fence, she could set it on fire. Once started, the dry brush and dead snags and green pine needles would flame like grass on the prairie. All of Blanding's hands, even if they were on the spot, could not put it out.

Lark's pain eased away with the surety of freedom for the horses, and only the dark, set mood remained. She knew exactly what she was going to do. Consequences of possible detection did not influence her.

Sunset in the west greeted her from the summit of the ridge, a sinister, black-streaked crimson, somehow harmonious with this day. The sage on that side stretched away, rose and purple. Her keen gaze swept along the mountain, at the indented slopes, and the bulge and heave of rougher country. If the wild horses once got on that side of the ridge they would take a great deal of catching. She calculated that if she could let them out of the trap without the help of fire they would travel up and over the slope.

The cowboys, with Coil Bruce ahead, caught up with Lark just as she reached camp.

"Rotten mess, wasn't it?" asked Coil.

"It sure was," she replied. She was not inclined to talk, but she saw that she could best avert further attention by being as civil and natural as possible. At the moment she caught sight of Bruce's lasso tied on his saddle. She would need that or one like it.

"I'll take your horse," offered Bruce, as Lark dismounted in front of her tent.

"Thank you, I'll look after him."

Lark took good care to observe where Bruce threw his saddle, so that she could locate it later. What to do with Chaps was a problem. If she hobbled him as usual and turned him loose it would not be easy to find him. After unsaddling him, she let him drink and then tied him to the tree behind her tent. Chaps did not care for this at all. She appeased him, presently, with a nose bag of oats.

Dusk fell. Marigold and her friends came riding in, clamorous though tired. Lark did not see Stanley. No doubt he was disgusted enough never to come back to camp at all.

Jeff's call to supper brought the girls and boys scurrying out. Stanley came from his tent. They appeared to be a starved lot, except Stanley, who puttered with his food and left the table early. And it was not to start up the campfire, as had been his habit. He disappeared. Lark did not see him again. But she watched the cowboys eating with Jeff at the chuck wagon and she was careful to count them, and to identify Bruce. Then from her tent she glided back in the gloom, and, finding the place where Bruce had left his saddle, she soon had the coveted lasso in her possession.

Chaps had eaten all of his oats and manifested a desire for more, or to be released. Lark did not want to be seen getting more grain. Neither did she want Chaps to neigh around camp. Therefore, under cover of the darkness she saddled and bridled him again, and led him up the ridge for a distance and haltered him to a tree. Chaps was well trained. This was all right with him, evidently, as it meant that Lark intended to ride again. She remained with him awhile, petting him, and then she hurried back to camp.

A big fire blazed brightly. Lark did not join the camp-fire circle. She sat on her bed, with the tent flaps open, and watched. Stanley was not among the group. He had gone to bed, no doubt, and was now lying in misery, try-ing to fathom his problem. Lark gave her conjectures free rein.

Lark drew a blanket about her. If it had not been for Chaps she would have gone to bed, to lie awake for hours. But she waited patiently until the campfire circle showed signs of breaking up for the night. Then Lark slipped out and stealthily stole up the slope. In a few mo-ments she was beyond detection and breathed freer.

Chaps whinnied at her approach, which caused her to make haste. They were not yet out of range of the sharp-eyed cowboys. She hesitated before mounting. She had gloves, matches, lasso, but she had forgotten her sombre-ro. Presently she mounted, to head Chaps down the slope.

The night was dark, still, cold. The moon would not be up until hours later. The valley below appeared like a black hole, locked in silence. Far down to the left flick-ered the campfires of Blanding's outfit. They would be making merry over the day's prize. They would not be merry in the morning.

Chaps found the trail. It was soft and grassy, giving forth no sound under his hoofs. Below, Lark remem-bered, near the trap she would need to dismount and go very carefully, to avoid making a noise.

As she proceeded, the state of cool pondering alternat-ing with suspense which possessed her gradually under-went a change. It dawned upon her finally what she might expect if she fell into Blanding's hands. But she would have to be caught by his riders first. The possibility seemed remote. Blanding might send a few men to stay all night near the trap, though Lark considered that doubtful. If it did happen, however, these men would undoubtedly camp outside of the gate, and this would put them a quarter mile from Lark's objective. In case of a surprise Lark thought grimly that she could shoot her way out. She would not mind taking a shot at Blanding anyhow. Her father had not been a man who ever hesitated to use a firearm. But killing a man, except in defense of her life or honor, was unthinkable. Lark felt extremely dubious about using a gun in the dark upon moving men. Yet she had to go on, risk or no risk, and she did not intend to be caught.

After traveling a couple of miles she drew Chaps to a walk, and soon after that she reached the dark boulder which marked the line for her to descend. It was gray and gloomy down there in the notch. No fires! She had to strain her ears to catch sounds of horses. They were there, apparently resting. Lark, assuring herself that her enterprise was favored by fortune, rode down very slowly.

At length she got as far as she needed to go, if she intended to slip down on foot to reconnoiter, and make sure whether or not Blanding had sent a man back. But, after all, what good would it do her to know whether they were there or not? In any case she meant to liberate the horses. She would waive that added work, and proceed under the assumption that Blanding's riders were there.

Dismounting, she walked a little apart from Chaps to listen. First she heard the low fall of water, then the light steps and thuds of hoofs of uneasy horses. She was about a hundred yards above the fence, even with the center, where she meant to make the break. Next she heard an owl hoot, and after that the whine of coyotes. They were down in the trap attracted by dead horses.

Lark returned to Chaps and, taking up his bridle, slipped her hand up almost to the bit and led him very cautiously, a few slow steps at a time. Soon she was in the section where it would be easy to crash brush, crack a stick or roll a rock. She bent low, searching the ground, and it was certain that she made no sound which could have been heard many yards away. It took precious time to do this. She realized that, at the last, when she tied the lasso to the trees in order to snake them out and open up the fence. Noise would be unavoidable. Then, however, it would not matter so much, for she could drag three trees out of there in less than three minutes and be gone. But she had forgotten that she must also light the fire.

As she worked down most carefully she turned these

things over and over in her mind. And the result was that she elaborated a safer and better plan.

The thicket, which she soon entered, was dark, and the way tortuous. Pine saplings and brush of a leafless variety crowded upon her. The ground was thick with pine needles. This place would burn fircely; in fact, the whole brushy slope above the fence would go. There was no other plot of timber near, something she had noted before deciding on this hazardous venture. The wild-horse catchers would have to travel far to find more material for a new fence.

At last Lark was down, close to the high line of piled trees and brush. A cleared lane, which the riders had cut, offered Lark room to drag out the large bushy treetops she had selected. She made sure that they were the right ones. Then, going beyond them, she gathered armloads of pine needles and dry bits of dead wood, which she piled against the fence.

That done, she was ready. But she waited longer to listen. In that interval she discovered that she was panting; her face was bathed in cold sweat; she felt a tingling and thrilling of nerves. Sounds disturbed her. The wild horses were restless. They scented her or Chaps. She heard them moving inside the fence. How could she be sure those steps were not made by men?

The moment had come. With firm hands Lark tied one end of the lasso round the first tree she had selected. Then she got on Chaps, and winding the other end round the pommel she spurred him. He gave a lunge; the rope tightened. The tree rustled loud, branches cracked. Lark's heart leaped high, her tongue clove to the roof of her mouth. She heard wild horses snort inside the fence. They were curious. She saw dark heads pointed up against the background of gray. Chaps appeared to be stuck. She spurred again and beat him with her glove. He plunged, dug down, and straining hard he loosened the tree with a crash and got it moving. Momentarily it caught on the second tree, but this one started too, and presently the sturdy little mustang dragged them both out.

Lark leaped off and flew back. Her hands were not

steady now when she untied the rope. A gray aperture broke the solid outline of the fence. Lark dragged Chaps across this opening to tie on to the third tree. This was wide and bushy, but it came more easily. Its removal left a gateway wide enough to drive through two wagons abreast. It was enough. Just inside wild horses edged close, snorting. Suddenly a gray beast with the whites of his eyes showing broke through the opening.

Lark had to leap to escape him. Then Chaps plunged and dragged her. More horses bolted through. When she got the frightened Chaps under control a stream of them was pouring out of the break. They did not make a great deal of noise, but even that added to Lark's fright. Nor did they crash the brush, for the reason that the great mass of horses had not yet started. But she heard a quick trampling of hoofs all along the inside of the fence, up to the apex of the trap. They would not rush the break. They were coming steadily, stamping, snorting, but not wild with terror. That sliding, dark stream seemed uncanny.

Watching spellbound, Lark, in the intensity of her feeling, forgot for the moment her own danger. Yet instinctively she had made ready to mount and flee.

The sight of the wild horses coming thicker and faster, pouring out like oil, worked Lark to a pitch of joy. She had opened a way for them and she could have screamed. The odor of dust and sage and horses floated to her. The slithery sounds of bodies rubbing together, the knock of hoofs and the scattering of gravel confirmed the moving column in her blurred eyesight. Oh, go on—go on! Make way for those behind! Hurry, you blacks and grays and browns! Freedom! The wide sage lies yonder—the safe heaven of your hill—the distant range! Point your noses straight and low, you lean, wild shaggy darlings! Run—run—run!

They might have heard Lark's inward cry. They gained momentum; they came thicker; they poured out in a swift column. Lark dragged her mustang farther back from the widening stream. Dust choked her. The break grew gray, through which dark forms, like ghosts, shot on endlessly.

Then the rush and pound passed by her, up the slope, waving away, growing softer every moment.

Lark jerked out of her trance. The murky gateway she had made no longer showed weird shadows through the dust. The wild horses had arisen to her silent call. They had poured out in one long swelling line. They were gone. From far up the slope floated down the last low, rushing sound.

Only one thing wanting now! She ran to light the pile of tinder. How it blazed up! It showed the great gap in the fence, now shadowy with yellow dust. Lark leaped upon Chaps and spurred him up the slope out of the widening circle of light. Fearfully she gazed back. The brush fence was crackling; the flames shot up red and leaping; the sparks floated high. She could see down into the trap. Empty save for dead horses dotting the gray! No sound save the crackle of wood, the increasing low roar of flame! She gained the level of the first bench, where she had left the trail. All seemed well. Her heart was not behaving. It felt too big, too tumultuous for her breast.

It was done. She reveled in the deed. Her elation gained on her fears, on the sustained suspense that now broke, leaving her weak. What a terrible flare behind! It lit up the wide notch; it would make the whole valley like day. She must hurry; yet she ought not hurry. She would unsaddle Chaps far back of camp and carry her saddle down to her tent. She would be in bed when the alarm came. Suddenly she made a discovery. The lasso was gone. She had lost it. She remembered coiling it and hanging it over the pommel, but she had not tied it. She dared not go back. Suppose it were found and recognized! But she would not let Bruce suffer for her work.

Thrilling hot and cold, her mind whirling, Lark rode on up the trail. Soon she would pass the big rock on the corner and be out of the light. For that fence was now a long red torch. The slope, too, was on fire.

Suddenly Chaps reared to come down with a thud. He snorted. Lark saw a tall, dark form slide out of the shade into the trail. Her heart seemed to burst and send a hot gush of blood throughout her body. She reached for the gun.

"Lark! It's Stanley. Don't be frightened," spoke a low, sharp voice. She recognized the ring of it.

"Oh—Stanley!" she gasped, and then she almost collapsed.

He put a reassuring hand on the shaking mustang. "Chaps, old boy. Steady now. Don't you know me?"

"I—I didn't know you—till you spoke," faltered Lark. "Oh Lord, I was scared."

"Lark Burrell, you've played hell," he said, coming close to her.

"Have—I?" she asked almost wildly.

"You bet you have. But we mustn't talk here on the trail. Somebody will see the fire and come running."

He took the bridle from her and, leading Chaps, started off the trail straight up the slope. The huge boulders and big pines presently eased Lark's reawakened fright. How lucky for her that it had been Stanley she encountered! He was short, cold, angry. She watched him, speculating on what he would say. That did not matter. He certainly would not betray her. Anyway, the wild horses were free.

Far up on the ridge top Stanley halted. "Get off," he said.

She obeyed. With swift hands he threw the saddle and bridle. A slap sufficed to send Chaps off. Lark then observed that the moon had arisen from behind the mountain.

"I'll pack your saddle down later, when it's safe for us to risk it," said Stanley. "Now—you damn little fool, what have you done?"

"What do you think?" asked Lark flippantly. If he wanted to be like that—let him.

"I think you've been idiot enough to burn Blanding's fence."

"You've got me wrong, Stanley. I've been *man* enough to let those wild horses out and then burn the fence."

"But, my heavens, girl! It'll ruin you," he declared, spreading his hands wide. He was distressed.

"Ruin me? How can you ruin a girl who is nobody, has nothing—not even a name?" she asked.

"You're mistaken. You have a name. A good name."

"Well, if you tell on me that'll be gone sure," she said.

"*Tell* on you? Good God, Lark, how can you think such a thing?"

"How'll I be found out and disgraced unless you do tell? . . . But that's nasty, Stanley. I'm a little out of my head. I know you'd never betray me."

"Someone will find out. It's just our luck."

"*Our* luck?" she echoed, marveling that he bracketed her with himself.

"I said that, Miss Burrell."

"Are you angry, Stanley?"

"Angry? I'm seeing red, right now. I ought to spank you."

That idea ought to have been funny, but it was not. He looked so big and strong and fierce; now and then as he moved, the moonlight pierced the foliage of the pine, and shone white on his face. His eyes burned on her. This accelerated her heart another way, and already she had withstood enough from that uncertain member.

"I'm not a child to spank," she managed.

"You are, by thunder. Now, tell me just what you did after we left that trap this afternoon, so I can judge what chance we have of beating this."

She told him the essentials.

"You stole Bruce's lasso and lost it!" he exclaimed.

"I did."

"Well, I'll have to go find it. You stay here," he said brusquely.

"You will not." She threw out a hand to catch his arm. "I wouldn't let you risk that. Suppose Blanding sees the fire and rides up there!"

"You're right. It'd be risky. But that rope will be found."

"It might not be. I think I dropped it between the fence and the thicket. Surely it'll be burned."

"Lark, if that rope is found Bruce or some of our cowboys will be accused. It's serious. There will be a fight."

"I can stop that."

"How?" he asked, bending over her, and grasping the hand she had put on his arm.

"I'll confess."

"Lark! You shall do nothing of the kind."

"Sure I will. What do I care? Blanding can't do anything to me. Let him have me arrested. I'll bet I could make any sheriff let me go."

"But I care. You shall not do that. Promise me." He gave her a most decided shake.

Lark's rebellious spirit had had too much to contend with lately. His look was worse than his violence, and the intimation that he cared played more havoc than both.

"I—I promise, Stanley."

"Very good. That'll help. You're to keep absolutely quiet about this. No matter what happens—who comes to our camp. Understand?"

"I'll keep quiet," she replied, thinking how wonderful he looked as he loomed over her. He was gazing down at her most compellingly. He was terribly concerned about this predicament into which she had gotten herself.

Suddenly Stanley took her in his arms and drew her up clear to her tiptoes, till her breast was hard against his. So astounded was Lark that she sank heavily to him. Her head fell back to lodge against his left arm which encircled her neck. His other arm was low about her waist, and so tight Lark could not breathe properly.

"Why—Stan-ley!"

"Why what?" he asked, and now all the sternness was gone from his voice.

"Why—what do—you mean?"

"I don't know yet. . . . But you're a wonderful girl. A real Western girl, like my mother was. Like my grandmother, who rode the Oregon trail before she was eighteen."

"Thanks, Stanley. . . . That's nice, but—it's no—no reason to do this," she remonstrated. She could not move. She did not want to—that was the sudden realization.

"Well, there's more. You've got a heart and soul. You've got nerve, Lark. In addition to all that, you're wonderful."

Then Lark realized something was terribly amiss. She began to tremble. "Please let me—go."

"Not much."

"But this isn't—right—or—or fair of you, Stanley."

"No? Isn't it nice, though?" he went on tantalizingly.

"If it is—you shouldn't—say so."

He bent closer, and swayed her so that the moon shone on her face. His piercing eyes robbed her of what little strength she had left.

"You owed me a kiss, didn't you?"

"Yes, but Stanley—d—you don't want it now."

"I've got to have it. Remember now. You won the bet, but you promised just the same. And it must be a real kiss, all of your own accord. None of your pecks on the cheek, like I saw you give Marigold. Will you pay up now?"

"I can do no less—if you insist," she faltered.

"Lark, I don't insist. I command you to pay your debt, as I intend to pay mine."

He bent his head. Lark had a fleeting sense of the imminence of calamity. She raised her face—pressed her lips to his. Something swept through her—shock—sweetness—lightning. She meant to pay fairly, even good measure, but her lips clung. Her eyelids drooped involuntarily, the bright moon vanished, she seemed to float away.

It was Stanley who drew away, shocking her to actuality.

"There," she whispered shyly. "Now—let me go."

"After that? Never!" he retorted wildly. And then he kissed her. "Lark, you darling!"

"Stanley, are you mad?" she cried, trying to free herself.

"Quite mad. Gloriously mad . . . Mad with the nectar of love . . . Lark, kiss me again."

"Oh, Stanley, let me go," she wailed, suddenly awakening.

His answer was to kiss her lips again, and then her cheeks, her eyes, her forehead, her hair, and once more her mouth. When he stopped Lark made one single passionate struggle. Strength came back. She fought him while her shame and scorn and fear found vent.

"Are you another Blanding? . . . How dare you, Stanley! . . . Oh, I thought better of you than this. . . . To take advantage of—my weakness for you . . . You're a—a cheat!"

"Listen," he interrupted, clasping her tighter, so that she could neither move nor breathe. He was so appallingly strong.

"Wait, you hurt—me," she gasped faintly. "You'll break something. . . . I can't get—my breath."

"Very good, then. Will you stop fighting?" he returned, loosening his hold.

"Yes. But oh!"

"Lark, I love you," he said in tender passion. "Say you love me."

"No—no! I won't. I don't. I—I hate you. . . ."

"But, darling, is it so very wicked of me to love you—when you're the very sweetest and dearest of girls in all this world?"

That loving epithet from his lips stabbed Lark afresh. "Oh, you do not—l-love me! You've just lost your mind. The day—tonight—it's no wonder. I forgive you, Stanley. But let me go—I beg you."

"Can't you get it through your pretty little dark head? I *do* love you. I *have* loved you ever since that very first day. Now what?"

"Oh, it's madness, I tell you," cried Lark. To resist him, to try to think of Marigold, was horrible.

"Well, if we're both mad, what's the difference? Kiss me again, darling," he said in gay tenderness, bending slowly as if to make her see his intention, to force her subjugation. If he kissed her that way again she was doomed. And he did. Lark broke then.

"Oh—help me, heaven. I do love you. . . . Oh—S-Stanley—no more . . . I implore you . . . mercy—mer—"

He would not be denied. And another Lark Burrell, who had been storming her conscience, rose up in her triumphantly, rapturously, to clasp him round the neck and give him the kisses that the other Lark had denied. Then she grew limp and faint.

"Why, Lark!—Here, honey, I've been a little precipitous," he burst out in great concern. "Come, let's find a seat on the rock. I'm sorry, dear. I was afraid if I didn't make a flying start and hold on that you'd get away."

He supported her to a seat on a flat stone under the pine, and there Lark lay against his shoulder, spent and surrendered, most miserably happy and bewildered.

"Now, Stanley, it's you who has played hell," she spoke up presently.

"Me? I don't think. *I* have played heaven. At least that's where I am."

"How can you be so heartless? Are all men like that? I'm beginning to believe some of the things these other girls say. . . . If you honestly and truly love me—oh, it's too wonderful and terrible to believe!—there're going to be two broken hearts."

"Whose?"

"Marigold's and mine . . . What a guilty wretch I am! —Stanley, how did you ever come to love me?"

"Simple enough. Anybody would. Marigold does, despite her jealous nature . . . And, darling, you've forgotten that I'm free."

"Oh, Stanley! But we can't give in to it."

"What do you mean, Miss Burrell?" he asked loftily. "That's a queer statement. I'll have you understand my intentions are honorable."

"Oh! . . . You—I—Stanley," she floundered helplessly, feeling the hot blood rush up to her temples.

"I know what you meant, darling," he laughed.

"Is it honorable to make me give in—when you—you know Marigold will make up with you?" she asked gravely.

"Honorable all right, honey. Marigold broke it off. But I'm bound to admit this is in rather indecent haste. I meant to wait until we got back to town. But heavens, Lark, consider. Be reasonable. *I* slipped out tonight on the identical job you performed."

"*Stanley!*" she cried, leaping up to face him in the moonlight. "You meant to free the wild horses?"

"You bet I did."

"Oh, bless you! . . . That finishes me." And she threw her arms around his neck. That was the last straw. She would worship him now. Nothing else—nobody else mattered to her. It had been enough to love him, to plan to go home and dream the rest of her life away, true to him, but since the incredible had come to pass, since he too had fallen from grace to love her, then he could do with her as he willed.

Stanley freed her gently and stood up.

"I hear yelling," he whispered. "Listen."

She awoke to apprehension. Yes, she heard shouts of men.

"Hear that, Lark? I can't tell where they come from. But we'd better defer this hour until some more propitious time. Come."

Without another word he stepped over to where her riding accouterments lay, and, putting the saddle blanket and bridle on the saddle, he shouldered the load and strode off. Lark, dizzy and weak, ran after him, and caught his free hand. It closed over hers reassuringly. They walked on down the slope until the tents shone white in the moonlight. He halted to listen.

"Nobody up here," he whispered presently. "Those yells came from Blanding's men. Let 'em yell. Now, Lark, are you all okay?"

"I think so," she whispered.

"You go now. I'll follow with your saddle," he went on. "Don't make any noise. Keep behind the trees and rocks. Slip in your tent and go to bed. Tomorrow be as usual. And if anything turns up you don't know anything. Understand?"

"Yes. . . . Good night," she whispered.

"Good night, Lark darling," he returned.

Then she fled.

15

STANLEY DEPOSITED the saddle on the ground and sat down to watch and listen.

He saw Lark's dark form flit across the moonlit patches, at length to vanish round her tent. She was safe. Then he attended to other considerations. After a long wait he heard distant, sharp cries. Coyotes! That might have been what he had heard before. But Lark had agreed with him.

Behind him the sky appeared aglow. It was an effulgence from the burning brush. Long slants of smoke rose high above the pines. He watched until he thought there was a fading of the glow. Perhaps, however, that was due to the clouds obscuring the moon. At any rate a blight fell upon the ridge top. Taking advantage of this, Stanley shouldered his burden and went down the slope. He leaned the saddle against a pine near Lark's tent, and then, slipping round below, he crossed the brook to approach his tent from a different angle. Before entering it he listened once more. The night was still. He could hear one of the cowboys snoring. There was a horse somewhere near, and the wind had begun to moan. The sky was a dull red over the ridge.

At last he went into his tent, tied the flaps and dropped upon his bed, more spent than he had been after many a hard ride. But it was too cold, and he made haste to undress and get into bed, where he lay with chattering teeth for some moments.

What a day and a night! Worry clouded his bliss. There could never be any unalloyed joy. Lark's kisses still lingered on his lips and he would not have changed anything. How maddeningly sweet it had been to torment her, to work upon her feelings! He suffered remorse; yet he would have done the same thing all over again. Marigold, no doubt, had made greater his need of love and faith. What a nine day's gossip there would be in Wadestown presently! Stanley Weston rejected! And a terrible twisting of subsequent events, whatever they might turn out to be.

This was the second night in which he had lost much sleep. Nature rebelled and clubbed him into slumber. And when he awoke, after what seemed only a moment, there was gold sunshine upon his tent. Still he felt loath to begin this day. It presaged evil. Blanding was absolutely sure to lay the loss of those wild horses to him.

Jeff was whistling outside, and, as always, making numerous and unnecessary noises with tins, buckets, whatever came to hand. It was only in the early mornings, whenever everybody wanted to sleep, that he made any racket. Horses were whinnying. Someone swung a vigorous, ringing ax. It was high time Stanley got up. How marvelous it would be when he gazed into Lark's face this morning in the clear light of day! The thought dragged him quickly out of bed.

The sun had just topped the eastern sage flat—a glorious burst of rose. The nipping air smelled of burnt wood. It could not have come from Jeff's fire. Far up the ridge traces of smoke lingered, but he would not have noticed them had he been unaware of the fire last night.

When he went across to Jeff's for some hot water, he heard Coil Bruce call out: "Hey, Red, did you swipe my rope?"

"No, you durn fool. What'd I want your rope for?" returned Red testily.

Then Coil addressed Landy in much the same way, to be laughed at.

"Somebody stole my rope off my saddle," yelled Bruce, and went after Jeff. This fetched a guarded but prolific flow of profanity. Stanley could have used much the same himself, and anathematized Bruce for planting the idea of a lost rope in the minds of his comrades.

Soberly Stanley marched back with his pan of hot water and ponderingly applied himself to the task of shaving. He cut himself, too, and that did not improve his mood. After completing his ablutions he set about building the campfire, stealing the while many a glance at Lark's tent. But she did not show herself promptly. Marigold came out singing. She wore blue. Her hair caught the sunlight beautifully.

"Good morning!" she called cheerily to Stanley as she tripped to the fire.

"Good morning, Marigold!"

She stared at him. . . . "Say, you bloody man! Stan, have you tried to cut your throat?"

"No. I didn't take it that hard. I was shaving and nicked myself."

"Oh, that's it. I sort of had a hope you'd repented."

"My God!" ejaculated Stanley. "Can you beat that?"

The arrival of Marigold's other guests at the campfire precluded any more of this badinage, much to Stanley's relief.

Lark put in an appearance then. One glance at her reassured Stanley as to her state; he almost believed last night had been a dream. She gave him no glance at all, however, and on the way to breakfast, a wide berth.

"Where do we go today?" asked one of the girls insatiably.

"Who wants to see the wild horses roped and tailed and driven?" asked Marigold.

All except Lark gave eager affirmative. Marigold observed the omission.

"Well, coz, aren't you in on it?" she inquired sweetly.

"I had enough yesterday," replied Lark with composure.

"How about you, Stan?"

"Nothing doing," blurted out Stanley.

"You two tender lovers—of wild horses—can stay in camp today," said Marigold with a hint of irony.

"Thanks," returned Stanley dryly.

Marigold changed the subject. There was a good deal of merry chaffing during breakfast. Stanley kept up his end, but he was far from real mirth. Lark brightened perceptibly under Marigold's evident desire to make up for her coldness the day before. So, altogether, breakfast passed smoothly.

"Boss, when do you want the horses?" called Landy.

"No hurry, Landy," rejoined Stanley, avoiding Marigold's quick glance. He went to his tent. Later he made it a point to encounter Lark, just as she came round the corral, evidently having been tending Chaps. She had color in her cheeks. Only her eyes, suddenly those of a startled deer, checked Stanley's intent to tease.

"Full of pep this morning—you!"

"Oh, Stanley, she was sweet to me again," rejoined Lark earnestly.

"She. Who?"

"Marigold, of course. I think she was sorry. Oh, no one can help loving her."

"She can affect people, that's sure," replied Stanley with a laugh. "Did you catch that subtle remark of hers, about our being tender lovers—of wild horses?"

"Did I? She paused a long moment after—'lovers.' She had a laughing devil in her eyes. Stanley, something has changed Marigold."

"Humph. She's never the same two days running. She used to purr over me one day and tear my hair out the next."

"Seems to me she was suspicious of—of us—then rose above it. That hurts terribly—when we are both traitors."

"Look, if *we* are traitors, what was she?" asked Stanley deliberately.

She flushed scarlet. "No matter what she was, she's still—"

Landy Elm's sharp voice broke Lark off short.

"Hey, Stan, where are you?"

"Here. What you want?"

"Look! Hurd Blanding's on the ridge. He's on the way here."

"Lark, something doing sure," whispered Stanley hurriedly. "Better stay in your tent."

"Not much," retorted Lark, her eyes lighting.

"Keep quiet, then."

They separated, Lark hastening in the direction of her

tent. Stanley backed away so that he could look over the rocks. Sure enough, there came Blanding riding down the ridge. He was alone and in no hurry.

"Wonder what he wants," muttered Stanley.

"Probably feelin' his best after that big haul of hosses," replied Elm.

The men, except Bruce, all expressed opinions, none of them flattering to the wild-horse hunter, and Bruce looked dark. Stanley made a mental note that he would like to know why Bruce wore such a troubled face.

Blanding was riding down the trail above Lark's tent. He would undoubtedly pass by it and come into camp from that quarter. Wherefore Stanley strolled out toward the campfire, where Marigold, Doris, Evelyn and young Fairchild were getting warm.

"Marigold, have you any idea why Blanding should come to our camp?" inquired Stanley.

"What!" ejaculated Marigold blankly.

"There he comes, all right," declared Stanley, not without grimness.

Marigold whirled to see the rider approaching. For one instant she was plainly startled, then recovered to express only surprise that was genuine.

"Wonder what he means—butting in here. Must be serious," she said, as if thinking aloud.

Stanley saw Lark, who had just sat down in the camp chair in front of her tent.

Blanding halted his horse at the brook opposite Lark's tent. He made a superb figure on his big mount. He addressed Lark, but in so low a tone that Stanley could not catch what he said. She gazed at him steadily, without replying. At that moment Stanley, at least, sensed something deep and hostile in Lark's gaze.

Blanding laughed aloud, with a kind of steely, hard ring. He leaped his horse across the brook, heading, however, to the right of the campfire, toward Bruce and the other hands who had come curiously out.

Stanley, of course, knew that Blanding had not ridden over to make a pleasant morning call. But why did he come alone? Stanley took time to search the ridge top for other riders, and not in vain. Far up the slope, almost out of sight, the heads of horses and men showed over the line of sage. What was Blanding's game? He reined in and leaned an elbow on his pommel. His chaps, corduroys and boots showed hard wear. He packed a bone-handled gun in a belt. His white flannel shirt, obviously donned that morning, showed off his fine physique. His profile was clean-cut, cold, as if chiseled out of stone.

He did not, apparently, notice Stanley and the group at the fire.

"Any of you punchers lose a rope?" he asked tersely, without any greeting.

"I did," replied Coil Bruce, stepping out.

"That it?" went on Blanding, taking a lasso off his pommel.

"Nope, too dirty. Mine was new," replied Bruce. "Much obliged all the same."

Stanley knew what was coming and his nerve leaped with his swift thoughts to meet this situation. He walked out a few steps.

"Have a look, anyhow," said Blanding, tossing the rope over.

Bruce caught it, gave the end a graceful pitch, after the manner of cowboys with a lasso. It was clean in part, black in others. He drew in the loop, suddenly startled.

"Sure this's my rope, Blanding," he said curiously. "I'd know my knot in a thousand. But how'n h—how'n the dickens did it get burnt like this?"

"Search me," replied Blanding laconically. "Maybe you dropped it yesterday and—"

"No, sir," interrupted Bruce, astounded. "That rope was on my saddle when I took it off last night. This mornin' I missed my rope. . . . Fellows, didn't I rave about it?"

"Reckon you did," admitted Landy.

"Sure, we all heard you," put in Jeff.

"You'd swear it was on your saddle last night?" went on Blanding, still cool and slow, as if the matter was not particularly important.

"Yes. I know it was—positively," declared Bruce.

"Then you used it last night," flashed Blanding, as if unmasking a battery.

"What!—I did nothin' of the kind. I never left camp. . . . Somebody stole—"

It was not an interruption that halted Bruce's hot speech. Suddenly he seemed to have encountered an inhibiting thought.

"Listen, you bozos," blazed Blanding, his voice rising to passion. "This rope of Bruce's was used last night to snake trees out of my trap fence."

"It's a damn lie!" burst out Bruce fiercely. "If it *was* used, you're the one who stole it from my saddle."

"Hell! That'll go fine in court," returned Blanding.

"Blanding, you've been sneakin' around our camp at night. I *saw* you," shouted Bruce, red in the face.

"Ha ha! It wasn't to steal ropes, my bucko."

Stanley took a single stride that was a start as well. "Coil, are you on the level? Did you honestly see Blanding around our camp, after dark?"

"You bet I did. I'll swear to that."

Blanding turned with a sneer on his handsome face. He was pale and his eyes were like molten steel.

"Weston, you're behind this," he rasped.

"Behind what?"

"What! You know damned well! The plot to ruin my drive. This rope of Bruce's was used to snake trees out of our fence. It was opened up. *Every horse let out!* The——who used this rope lost it. And there you are!"

"Is that so?" asked Stanley sarcastically. "Well, if you've got to get it off your chest, do it without curses. There are ladies here."

"I'll cuss till I'm black in the face, Weston. You can't get away with this deal. Somebody in this outfit has robbed me of ten thousand dollars. I can prove it. And by God, I'm going to get even."

With that he turned in his saddle, and, cupping his hands round his mouth, he yelled piercingly, *"Hey, Howard, fetch the gang down!"*

An answering shout preceded the rapid approach of riders.

"Hurd, this is an outrage," burst out Marigold.

"Ha, you bet it's an outrage," he retorted. "And if you've got sense enough to know what's good for *you*, you'll not butt in."

"Marigold, you and the girls go to your tents," ordered Stanley, raging now to see that Lark had come over, and was standing close, white and big-eyed.

"No. We'll be in this, whatever it is. Let me talk to Hurd," replied Marigold resolutely.

"Go ahead and talk, if you must," said Stanley. "But it seems to me that Mr. Blanding doesn't care to hear you."

"Hurd," cried Marigold appealingly.

Blanding bent over in his saddle, his great, flaring gray eyes hard as flint. "Marigold Wade, do you want me to drag you into this?"

"What?" exclaimed Marigold, suddenly white.

"Don't what me," he retorted. "I'm beholden to you. And I'm trying to remember it. But don't try to save Weston. If you do I'll take it that you and your whole outfit of tenderfeet were in this dirty deal to loose my horses. And that means court."

For once, and the only time Stanley ever saw her so, Marigold was not only silenced but frightened. Stanley looked no more. Pity edged for a moment into his fury. Next moment he was steeling his nerve afresh, to meet this mob of hard riders galloping right into camp. The horses sent water and mud flying. The girls screamed and ran back, except Lark, who held her ground. These riders, fifteen or more, some of them swarthy Indians in white man's ragged garb, lined up behind Blanding. Ellery Wade rode in last, purple of face, to sit his horse and shake a fist at Stanley.

"You're gonna get yours, Stan Weston," he bawled furiously. "You're back of this job. . . . All our horses gone! Trap burnt! . . . Every dollar I had sunk in this drive! If we don't *hang* you, it won't be my fault!"

"El, for God's sake, don't be an idiot!" shrieked Marigold.

"Get back, Wade," ordered Blanding. "I'll do the talking here. . . . Weston, we've got the goods on you. Just agree to come across with ten thousand dollars, if you want me to let you off."

Stanley laughed scornfully in his face. Nevertheless it was rage and bluff, for this seemed assuredly no laughing matter. But what could Blanding prove? What card had he up his sleeve? What if by any chance he could implicate Lark in this grave situation?

"You turn that down?" demanded Blanding harshly.

Here Howard interposed, his expression one of malignant revenge. "We've got it on you, Weston!"

"Bah! You've got nothing on me," returned Stanley contemptuously. "Do you suppose any court would—"

"It'll never get into court," interrupted Blanding fiercely, waving Howard to keep silent.

"Well, it's nothing to me."

"Ahuh . . . Maybe *this* will be," snapped Blanding. And suddenly he drew from his pocket a scarf. The bright scarf Stanley had given Lark! Stanley's heart sank.

Blanding shook the scarf at Stanley. "Yesterday this scarf was around Lark Burrell's neck!"

"Sure. I lent it to her. It was returned to me when we got back from the ride," said Stanley coolly.

"It's yours then?"

"Yes."

"Fellows, you all hear that. He admits this scarf is his."

"I'll say we hear," replied Howard, with a hoarse haw-haw.

Blanding flipped out the scarf with shaking hands. "Aha! Stan, old top, what have we here! . . . See. Two holes burned in this necktie you gave your little Lark! One of my Indians found it on a green bush, only partly burned. . . . Found it this morning—down there—not twenty feet from where my brush fence ran."

His intensity radiated from him like heat from a furnace. He had more than this to reveal. Stanley divined that in sickening certainty.

"Now what do you say?" resumed Blanding.

"You've got the goods on me," replied Stanley calmly eying his accuser, and measuring the distance between them. Stanley was about ready for some action, gun or no gun.

"Ho! Ho! Ho!" roared Blanding in fiendish glee. "Hear that, boys? He admits that, too."

"Damn you, Stan Weston, you've got to settle with me," yelled Ellery Wade in exultant rage.

"Come across, boss," added Howard, his yellow eyes popping.

"Weston, will you pay for your little fun?" asked Blanding, growing husky.

"Not a dollar."

"I'll have you strung up!"

"Bunk!"

"I'll take it out of your hide."

"You'll *what?* Why, you big-eyed, straight-nosed, pretty horse killer, if you step down I'll put your beauty on the blink."

Blanding did not accept the invitation.

"We'll hog-tie you and horsewhip you," he thundered.

"There's enough of your cheap outfit to do that, I guess, but some of them will get broken bones."

"Hurd, you're stallin'," shouted Howard angrily. "You're playin' this out to dazzle the women. Tell him the rest straight—or I will."

"Weston, we've got more and worse on you," warned Blanding.

"Well—is that so!"

"We found little boot tracks down there—made late last night, according to the Indians."

"Did you?" asked Stanley in cold disdain.

"Sure did. These tracks came from Lark Burrell's boots."

"How do you get that?"

"The tracks were made by cowboy boots. The smallest size."

"Indeed. Well, what's that got to do with Miss Burrell?"

"She's the only one who'd attempt it."

"Who told you?" flashed Stanley, holding back.

"No less than Marigold Wade, the lady who's going to marry you—presumably. If she doesn't change her mind."

"When did she tell you?" demanded Stanley icily.

"Oh, Hurd, for God's sake, be yourself!" cried Marigold furiously.

"Three nights ago," replied Blanding, deaf to her appeal.

"Where?"

"Not so far from this camp. Down by the last big pine tree, to be exact."

Stanley felt a terrible rage. He had almost reached his limit. Blanding's ominous front, backed by the gun Stanley feared he would use only too quickly, held the inevitable onslaught in abeyance.

"Blanding, I remember now how Miss Burrell came to leave those tracks," said Stanley, choking back everything to make one more plausible argument. "We were riding back yesterday, and on the way round your trap, she dropped a glove, and got off to pick it up. Chaps didn't like being so close to the fence. He was skittish. I was about to ride back to help her when she caught him. Then before mounting she tightened her cinch. That will explain those tracks."

"You expect me to believe that!" cried Blanding with deadly insolence.

"Haw! Haw! Some smooth guy, Hurd," laughed Howard. "What do you suppose he'll say about the other afternoon, when the Indians seen him with this same little girl?"

"God only knows," replied Blanding in disgust. "But if you spill that, I'll gamble he'll have to say a whole lot to explain it to Miss Marigold Wade."

Stanley took a leisurely, casual step forward, then another.

"Blanding, I'll change my mind—to get rid of this disgusting scene," he declared. "If you'll go at once, without another word of this rotten framing, I'll meet your demands."

"Okay!" ejaculated Blanding, in reluctant satisfaction. "Howard, shut up."

"I will like hell. Not unless you agree to give me half that money."

"Man, you're crazy!" shouted Blanding, enraged again.

"Here goes. . . . Weston, our Indian, Nesspelly—he speaks good English—saw you with this Burrell girl in your arms—"

Stanley launched himself as of yore. As he alighted on thumping feet, close to the rearing horse, he swung with terrible force, hitting Howard in the abdomen. Simultaneous with the sodden sound, Howard heaved clear out of his saddle and went crashing to the ground. The horse plunged out of Stanley's way, leaving the field clear and Blanding in reach.

"Lay off me, you—!" he yelled in wild alarm.

Stanley's intention was obvious. But Blanding's laying a hand on his gun changed it. Stanley seized his wrist.

"Let go that gun! I'll break your arm."

The horse reared in fright. The cowboys backed away with sharp ejaculations, the girls screamed.

"Weston, it's your mess," hissed Blanding.

Stanley hauled with savage passion, meaning to disable the man. But the saddle girth broke. And the tremendous force of Stanley's onslaught swung Blanding clear of the horse. It galloped away, kicking at the flapping saddle. Stanley let go of Blanding, as they both fell, and with marvelous swiftness clipped him a hard but glancing blow on the chin. It added to Blanding's momentum, landing him free of Stanley.

They were both quick; Stanley bounding erect, but Blanding jerking up only far enough to lean on his left hand. His right swept out with the gun.

"—— —— you, Weston!" he hissed in deadly calm. "You'll never slug another man!"

"Look out, Stan. He'll shoot!" called Landy Elm, his piercing voice clear above the hubbub.

Suddenly they all grew mute. Blanding was deliberate. His intelligence had grasped that this was self-defense. His big white jaw stood out, his hair stood up. His eyes were diabolical. He endeavored to steady the gun, now aligned with Stanley's body. But before he pulled the trigger a shot cracked out.

Blanding screamed like a wild thing in agony. The impact of a bullet spun him round, as the gun went flying.

He rolled back, glaring, his right arm flopping like the wing of a chicken.

"Stop, Blanding, or you'll be the man to get bored," cried Lark, as with quick, short steps she ran past Stanley to kick the gun aside. Suddenly she stooped to pick it up with her left hand. In her right, held low down, was a gun that smoked. Then she faced Blanding.

"You horse killer!" she said ringingly. "*I* let those horses out. *I* burned your fence. Stanley lied to protect me . . . . Now you get out of here, pronto!"

Blanding was a spectacle to behold. His realization that Lark Burrell had shot him took the insanity of violence from him. He sat with his left arm supporting his right, the sleeve of which was now red.

Lark then turned to the white-faced circle behind Blanding, and, slowly backing away, the gun extended, she spoke again: "Get him up—pack him away—or some of you'll get another dose of Idaho!"

They stared aghast, then fell off their horses to comply with her order. They surrounded Blanding, who began to bellow maudlinly. Two of them picked up the gasping Howard. Ellery Wade alone took no part in this hasty proceeding. His face was livid. The others were muttering and cursing. They fetched Howard's horse, still frightened, and threw the man like a sack across the saddle. Blanding was helped to mount. His haggard face, now bloody and dusty, his rumpled hair, his wild eyes, gave him a grotesque appearance. His jaw wobbled.

"Take your medicine," sang out one of his men. "You meant to do for Weston, didn't you? An' you got spilled by a girl. Quit your ravin'."

They rode off in a mass around him, one horse carrying double, down through camp.

In the silence that ensued, Lark handed Blanding's gun to Stanley, who had jerked out of his trance.

"Lark—you saved—my life!" he panted huskily.

She bent down to pick up the bright scarf which lay spread wide on the ground, the burnt holes showing. She folded this and put it in her pocket with the gun.

"I reckoned he meant murder, Stanley," she replied.

Marigold rushed up with a hand over her heaving breast, her face like paste. Manifestly she made a valiant effort to conquer her emotion. But before she succeeded she was big enough and human enough to embrace Lark before them all.

"You're a wonder, Lark," she shrilled, half crying, half laughing. "We hand it to you. Blanding would have killed Stan! Oh, what an awful mess!—El, you dirty little skunk! If this gets out we're all ruined. . . . We'll break camp and go home right now!"

16

THE CAMP was bustling with activity. Tents were coming down, bags being packed, the horses were having a feed of grain before the long trek home.

At the moment Stanley was helping Lark, who was on her knees trying to close a too tightly filled duffel bag.

"You're the clumsiest fellow," she complained, not quite sure but that Stanley's clumsiness was only a covert fumbling to get his hands on hers.

"Honey, I'm nervous," he explained. "Didn't I just come near being shot?"

"Don't talk about that!" exclaimed Lark, shuddering. She extricated two fingers from his. "Roll my bed. I'll close this bag."

He straightened out her blankets on the tarpaulin, and began to roll her pillow inside while she moved on her knees back to the duffel bag. Presently the operation of rolling the tarpaulin brought him bumping against her again.

"Throw me the rope," he commanded.

She reached over for it and handed it to him, then resumed her task.

"Darling, we'll need more blankets than these," he said, as casually as if he were talking about the grass.

"What!" Lark felt a tingling start that ran over her from head to heels. Then suddenly she grew still as a statue, only her eyes moving, and they dilated and opened wide.

"I'd freeze to death," he went on frankly, very businesslike with the ropes. "Is it as cold down in Idaho as it is here—nights and early mornings?"

"N-not q-quite—in the spring," she stammered.

"We're going to camp on the way down—you know."

"We—we are!" she whispered.

"That's what I said, angel child," he returned blandly. "Seems to me shooting up a camp sort of makes you thickheaded. . . . Of course we are!"

"Stanley, you're crazy," she burst out.

"Quite so. You see what your charms have reduced me to?"

"Oh, you're teasing me," she declared, suddenly relieved. But his impassive face, though it had not yet regained the healthy hue of its tan, harmonized with his strange talk.

"How soon can you be ready to start?" he asked calmly.

"Back to Wadestown? Why as soon as the rest of them. Sooner." She glanced over to see that the other girls had not progressed very far. Marigold at the moment was absorbed in her hand mirror, quite oblivious to all around her.

"Back to Wadestown nothing. I wasn't talking about that."

"What—then?"

"I mean our honeymoon."

Lark's hands suddenly became nerveless, and, as they were practically supporting her on the duffel bag, she fell over it most clumsily.

"Who's awkward now, Miss Burrell?"

She struggled up, and then, still on her knees, with a distance of not three feet between them, she gazed full at him, determined, in spite of the terrific tumult within, to see this queer talk of his through or end it.

"Stanley, what was it you said about a honeymoon?" she asked, her heart rising to her throat.

"When can you get ready for ours?"

"Ours!"

"Sure. Ours. Us. Yours and mine."

"You're going to—to—to marry me?"

"I am, if you'll have me. And, well, whether you'll have me or not."

"Stanley Weston, you'd give up Marigold—the sweetheart of your boyhood—just because you fell in love with *me?*"

"Well, darling, I would, in a minute. But fortunately it's not necessary. She gave me up first."

"Oh— But she'll—be sorry!"

He slipped his hand inside his vest pocket, and, drawing forth something, he extended it for her to see. There in his palm lay a thin band of gold and a sparkling diamond. She stared from it to him. Not teasing now! He was pale again, and his dark eyes were serious and intense.

"Marigold gave it back to me, didn't she?"

"Yes—but—" gasped Lark.

"So that's off, Lark."

"And you think Marigold is serious—really means it?" exclaimed Lark incredulously.

"Of course she means it—but even if she didn't—"

"Oh," cried Lark poignantly. "I've suffered the tortures of the damned."

"What for?"

"Because I thought you were making love to me when I was sure Marigold would change her mind. And I couldn't stop you—I couldn't help it. I wanted it. I loved it. . . . I gave in—and, oh, the shame of that."

"Lark, forgive me. Darling, how you look! Wasn't I sufficiently loverlike last night?"

She gazed at him speechlessly.

"I know, honey, that this is upsetting your plans terribly," he went on. "You wanted to go to work in Wadestown, save your money and then return to your place in

Idaho to fix it up, and go back to the old life. Now didn't you?"

"Yes. That was my plan."

"Well, I love you, and I have my plans. It'll hardly be necessary for you to go to work for anybody but *me*. Love and honor and obey! Will you?"

"I do."

"Oh glory!" He reached for her, then suddenly caught himself. "There'll be some gossip in Wadestown, believe me. But we don't care. We'll get married and beat it for Idaho on our honeymoon."

"W-when?"

"Tomorrow if not sooner."

Lark's brain reeled and there were other calamitous revolutions within her, both physical and mental.

"Oh, Stan-ley! So—so soon?"

"We'd avoid a lot of embarrassment, not to say worse. Suppose you put it off for a week. You know Marigold will tell it all the minute she gets home. You know El Wade. You know how cold and cutting Ma Wade can be. Could you hide in your room all day and all night? Wouldn't you have to sit at meals with them? And meet people?"

"Stanley, if happiness doesn't kill me—I will—tomorrow."

He bent his fine head. "Lark, you've saved me. . . ."

The rest of that breaking-camp task passed with Lark in a trance. After all she never fastened the duffel bag. It was Stanley who found things she had forgotten, and Coil Bruce who handed her her gloves and one spur.

Marigold left first, with four of her friends. That left two others, besides Lark, to go with Stanley. The wagon would follow with the camp equipment and extra horses, in the charge of the cowboys.

They were off and soon down upon the level sage. Stanley deflected from the road to avoid going near Blanding's camp, where there were signs of activity. When they got outside the point a long line of mounted Indians was visible riding to the west.

"They're going to stick it out," declared Stanley. "Well, here's hoping that herd or wild horses gets away. But I fear for them. If it weren't for the Indians!"

Lark was so lost in enchantment that she hardly grasped the significance of the riders. Straightway she forgot. The gray sage, sweeping by, brought tears to her eyes; its strong, sweet scent filled her nostrils to intoxication.

They rode to Wadestown in three hours, catching up with Marigold as they entered the town. He drew his horse up alongside hers.

"We're stopping for a few things," announced Marigold gaily. "Won't you join us?"

Lark smilingly shook her head, but the other two girls dismounted with alacrity.

"Marigold, hadn't you better spring your little surprise?" asked Stanley.

"Why so soon, Stan?" she retorted, with a blue dancing devil in her eyes.

"Well, I might spring one myself," he replied, laughing.

"All right then, I'll beat you to it. All's well that ends well!"

As Stanley rode away she waved a friendly hand to Lark.

"Oh, Stan, don't you just love her—anyhow?" cried Lark.

"I confess to a little ineradicable weakness," he replied.

"I'm glad—glad. I couldn't be happy—wholly—if you didn't. Don't you—"

"Lark, let me think of serious matters," he interrupted. "I've got to let you out of my sight in three minutes. It's darned hard."

She did not speak again during the short ride out to the Wade ranch.

"Here we are, and I've got it all figured," said Stanley gaily. "Now listen, precious—"

"Stan, did you call Marigold all the sweet names you call me?" broke in Lark jealously.

"Not all, Lark. Honest now, you big-eyed wonder! I never called her precious, and certainly never this that I'll

call you now. Sweetheart! . . . Now what have you? . . .
Well, listen. Don't tell anybody anything. I'll tell Dad, of
course. He'll be delighted. But don't you let Marigold
question you. Sure, if she asks you, tell her you like me
quite a lot." He smiled. "I'll go down early tomorrow
morning and fetch the parson, then ride out for you; I'll
be here about ten o'clock. Meanwhile, you have your
things packed. Marigold will be sleeping, so we can slip
out with your bags. That's all. You won't fail me?"

"No, Stanley."

"You'll be good?"

"Very good."

"Well, one last word—the most wonderful you can
think of. I won't see you for nearly twenty-four hours.
Say it, Lark!"

"Darling," she whispered shyly.

"That'll do, but I hoped you'd say 'husband.' I'll make
you say that tomorrow! So long."

He galloped away in a cloud of dust, leaving Lark
standing there bewildered.

This state did not leave Lark until the supper gong
sounded, at which time it gave way to trepidation. It took
Lark so long to fortify herself to face the Wade family
again that she was late. But it appeared she was not to be
embarrassed, at least at this time. Ellery Wade, of course,
was not present. Marigold was at her gayest. Certainly
she had not yet told her parents anything. Even Mrs.
Wade was graciously kind to Lark.

Marigold went upstairs with her arm linked in Lark's.
"I'll come in your room for a minute. Mine is a mess."

They entered, and Marigold was careful to shut the
door.

"Lark, I only half kept my word to Stan," said she. "I
spread the news of my broken romance—not the first
time, by the way—among my friends. But I'm not up to it
yet so far as Dad and Mom are concerned. Maybe tomorrow. She'll hear it quickly enough. Mom'll be furious.
She loves Stan."

"Cousin, aren't you making a terrible mistake?" It was
a strange thing for Lark to say in the light of what had

happened, but she could not yet grasp the fact that the affair between Stanley and Marigold was definitely ended.

"No. Stan and I would never have been really happy," replied Marigold sagely. "Besides, I've got myself in a bad situation, as you may have guessed. Lark, I lied to you about that little scene with Blanding in the parlor. Did you believe me?"

"Oh yes," murmured Lark. "At first I—I had evil thoughts. But I was only too happy to believe you."

"You poor little dear . . . Lark, you're wonderful. . . . Tell me, you are in love with Stan, aren't you?"

"I—I like him quite a lot," replied Lark, lowering her eyes.

"He's lucky!—Lark, let me tell you something! Stan loves you as he never, never loved me. . . . There, I thought that'd shock you. . . . Now one thing more, cousin. There'll be a lot of gossip. But there always is gossip. And nothing will come of this."

"Don't you think it'll be dreadful for everybody to know I shot Blanding?"

"Lark, that won't amount to anything," declared Marigold. "I stopped at his camp this morning on our way in. He's got a bad hole in his arm, but no bones were broken. They'd sent for the doctor. Hurd was resting easy. Pretty sick over the loss of the Horse Heaven Hill herd. I induced him to deny that you shot him."

"I'm sorry I—I had to," replied Lark poignantly. "But he'd have killed Stanley."

"You bet he would. Thank heaven you did it, Lark. As a matter of fact you've save us all—more than you dream of."

"That helps," said Lark, breathing deeply. "If only they'd stop that cruel wild-horse driving!"

"I like horses, but not as you do. You, Lark, you suffer agony. I could tell that. Forget about the wild-horse drives. Blanding will quit after he catches that bunch."

"Oh, he will! That's fine. Then he'll not go down to my range to drive my wild horses?"

"No, he won't!" declared Marigold. "But someone else will, Lark. You must reconcile yourself, or forget it. . . .

Now I must run and dress. We will not speak of these things again. Kiss me, Lark."

Next morning at ten o'clock Lark stepped into Stanley's buckboard and was whisked away, without anyone being aware of it. She was scarcely aware of it herself, so great was her transport.

"I've told Dad all about it." Stanley's voice was deep with happiness. "He's so pleased that it's given him a new lease on life. He'll welcome you with open arms when we get back."

At ten-thirty she was no longer Lark Burrell, but a bride. She felt immeasurably detached from her old self—someone transformed, fresh, rapt, unutterably grateful for the glorious future.

Stanley's first gift consisted of two rings, a wedding ring —he had to borrow the parson's wife's ring to marry Lark—and a diamond ring that made her think of fairies. Then they bought a huge wagonload of every imaginable kind of stuff for the ranch and sent it ahead with a driver. Late in the afternoon, with their own camping equipment, food, saddles and baggage in a light wagon, they started leisurely out on their honeymoon. It was to be at least a two-week trip and Lark wished it might be longer, anxious as she was to see her ranch.

Their last camp, made at sunset, was on a brook not far from the village of Batchford and about twenty miles from Lark's ranch.

"Some country, you can bet!" Stanley kept saying, to Lark's ever-increasing delight.

Next morning they were off before sunrise. They had overtaken and passed the big wagon the previous afternoon. When they reached the top of the divide four miles above Lark's home, Stanley stopped the horses. They looked and gazed.

"Well, there's nothing to it. Just grand! Beats old Washington all hollow. Lark, we're going to have two homes, one here and one back at Sage Hill, and we'll spend the winters here, the summers there."

"Oh—Oh—Oh!" was all Lark could say.

"What's that white, winding ribbon down there?" He asked, pointing.

"That's my brook."

"What's the long, shining river wandering away into the purple?"

"That's my Salmon River," replied Lark proudly.

"Why, Lark, this country is beautiful. It's lovely. You never told me it was like this. There's color. Not the endless monotony of gray sage, but green, red, black, white purple—all colors. And, oh, look at that mountain range!"

Stanley was soon to see Lark's lonely home at close hand. She had not exaggerated the wrack and ruin of the corrals, the sheds, the barns. The old cabin stood sturdily, but the roof was caving in, and the chimney had toppled. It had, though, a picturesqueness Lark had not known how to describe.

As they drove up, Jake emerged from the open door. To Lark he appeared the same short, old, grizzled and wrinkled, honest-eyed farm hand that he had always been —an amazing circumstance, for Lark had expected Jake, and everything else, to be strangely changed.

"Jake, oh, Jake!" she screamed, and she could not see him for suddenly dimmed eyes. "I've come home! We've fetched you a wagonload of things—and here's my husband!"

The old fellow leaned back against the log wall, as if staggered.

"Fer God A'mighty's sake, if it ain't my Lark!"

Lark ran wildly over the place, so wildly that Stanley, in order to keep up with her, had to resort to some of the speed for which he had once been famous.

The kittens were there, only grown; their mother purred proudly for Lark; old Tom rubbed against her legs. The chickens, the pigs, the cows and calves, the horses, all were there, only hungrier looking than ever. The wolf dog had rushed to welcome Lark, but he was slow to accept Stanley.

Out on the range the jack rabbits were thicker than

ever; the coyotes watched from the ridge tops; the straggling cattle dotted the green. And everywhere over the
sweeping, rolling rangeland roved small bands of wild
horses. Lark kissed her hands to them.

"You own a thousand acres here?" asked her husband
thoughtfully.

"We do," replied Lark archly. "What's mine is yours."

"That works both ways. Lark, does your range go
across the Salmon? Hardly, I'd say."

"My land is a triangle between the two brooks and the
river, with the wide end on the river."

"Let's fence it."

"Fence this land? Oh, I wouldn't like that. I hate
fences."

"So I have observed. You burned one down not long
ago. Very well then, let's fence only pastures. We'll irri-
gate. We'll build. We'll plant. And we'll throw, for a
starter, five thousand head of cattle out on the range."

"Oh, Aladdin!" she cried, rocking to and fro. "And to
think I almost never went to Wadestown!"

And so they tramped and rode, hand in hand, from one
point to another and back again, until the arrival of the
big wagon by late afternoon sent them racing to see how
Jake would take this unexpected manna.

Jake did not disappoint even the wildly enthusiastic
Lark, though he did express himself a little too profanely.
But he was a practical man. He set to work shingling the
cabin. And Stanley threw off his coat to help. Lark
cleaned out the living room. Like magic the day had
passed.

After dark Lark and Stanley sat beside the great stone
fireplace, where fur traders, trappers, hunters, Indians
and pioneers had sat before them.

The wind mourned, the old hollow, wild note under the
eaves, inexpressibly sweet and heart-moving to Lark. She
had heard that there as a child.

"Gee, that's some wind!" ejaculated Stanley. "For
desert wind for me!"

"You can hear the river, too," said Lark. "It's high
now."

"Tomorrow we'll go look it over."

They remained at the ranch ten days without knowing where the time went. And when they had to go, it delighted Lark to see how loath Stanley was to leave.

They lingered long on the divide, looking back. The white horses, at least, shone like bright glints down on the green. The brook and the river caught the light. How serene and lonely, how unspoiled this land! The mountain range bulged out of the desert, purple where the foothills heaved off the level, then streaked with red and gray, then a winding zigzag black, and at last the pure white of the peaks set against the blue.

ZANE GREY

WESTERNS THAT NEVER DIE

They pack excitement that lasts a lifetime.
It's no wonder Zane Grey is the bestselling
Western writer of all time.
Get these Zane Grey Western adventures
from Pocket Books:

_____ 82884 **ARIZONA AMES** $1.75
_____ 82896 **BOULDER DAM** $1.75
_____ 82818 **CODE OF THE WEST** $1.75
_____ 82692 **DEER STALKER** $1.75
_____ 82877 **FORLORN RIVER** $1.75
_____ 82883 **KNIGHTS OF THE RANGE** $1.75
_____ 82878 **ROBBERS ROOST** $1.75
_____ 82076 **TO THE LAST MAN** $1.75
_____ 82879 **UNDER THE TONTO RIM** $1.75
_____ 82880 **U.P. TRAIL** $1.75
_____ 82881 **WESTERN UNION** $1.75
_____ 82882 **WILDERNESS TREK** $1.75

POCKET BOOKS
Department ZG 4-79
1230 Avenue of the Americas
New York, N.Y. 10020

Please send me the books I have checked above. I am enclosing
$_____ (please add 50¢ to cover postage and handling for each order,
N.Y.S. and N.Y.C. residents please add appropriate sales tax). Send check
or money order—no cash or C.O.D.'s please. Allow up to six weeks for
delivery.

NAME_____

ADDRESS_____

CITY_____ STATE/ZIP_____

ZG 4-79

OLD MASTER OF
THE OLD WEST
MAX BRAND

**Thundering action that never quits—Max Brand
lets you have it just the way you want it.
For the very best in Western entertainment, get
these Max Brand titles, available from
Pocket Books:**

_____82890 BELLS OF SAN FILIPO $1.75

_____82893 DANGER TRAIL $1.75

_____82887 FIGHTING FOUR $1.75

_____82894 HUNTED RIDERS $1.75

_____82888 LONGHORN FEUD $1.75

_____82885 LONG, LONG TRAIL $1.75

_____82891 OUTLAW OF BUFFALO FLAT $1.75

_____82886 RAWHIDE JUSTICE $1.75

_____82892 REWARD $1.75

_____82889 SEVEN TRAILS $1.75

_____81751 SHOTGUN LAW $1.75

Stirring Westerns from CLAIR HUFFAKER